NOISY ALIEN COMMUNICATOR
and The Visible Spectrum

NAC Device Invented by:

Scott Armstrong a.k.a. BENT NOISE

Short Stories by:

Matt Bitonti

Jackrabbit

Robert V. Kilroy

Bertram Montiekowicz

Paradox M. Pollack

Frankford Publishing

Noisy Alien Communicator

and The Visible Spectrum

Short Stories by Various Authors

Frankford Publishing Number 1 - The Kilo Delta Papa Edition

© 2022 Frankford Publishing LTD.

All rights reserved. No part of this publication may be reproduced, stored in a retrieval system or transmited in any form or by any means, electronic, mechanical, photocopying, recording or otherwise without the prior permission of the publisher or in accordance with the provisions of the Copyright, Designs and Patents Act 1988 or under the terms of any licence permitting limited copying issued by the Copyright Licensing Angency.

Published by:
Frankford Pubishing

Philadelphia, PA 19135 USA
frankfordpublishing.com

Typesetting: Matt Bitonti

NAC Illustrations and Cover Design: Scott Armstrong

Further Illustration: Simon Adams

ISBN: 979-8-9872146-0-2

WARNING:

ANY HUMAN ATTEMPTING TO ASSEMBLE

AN OFFWORLD TONAL OSCILLATOR OR

"NOISY ALIEN COMMUNICATOR"

IS IN VIOLATION OF GALACTIC LAW!

AS A TIER-8 CIVILIZATION, SOL HUMANITY

IS DISCOURAGED FROM CONTACT

WITH OTHER BEINGS, ESPECIALLY USING DEVICES

DESIGNED BY THE INTERDIMENSIONAL OUTLAW

ALSO KNOWN AS: BENT NOISE.

FAILURE TO HEED THIS WARNING

RISKS ALL PENALTIES THEREIN,

UP TO AND INCLUDING SPECIES ERADICATION.

NAC PARTS LIST

Component Count: 21

Ref	#	Value
BT1	1	9V Battery_Cell Single-cell standard 9 volt battery
BT1	1	9V Battery_Cell 9-Volt Battery Connector A-656 534-232
C1, C4	2	47 uF Polarized capacitor A-5713 667-ECA-1EM470
C2	1	103 (0.01 uF) Unpolarized capacitor, small symbol A-1366 594-K103K10X7RF5UL2
C3	1	104 (0.1 uF) Unpolarized capacitor, small symbol A-214 594-K104K15X7RF5UL2
D1	1	Red LED 5 mm LED A-1554 638-333-2SDRTS5303
J1	1	PJ398SM-12 Mono Audio Jack (Optional) A-2563 (PJ-3001F) 490-MP3-3501
LS1	1	Speaker (8 ohm 1 watt should work) A-5725 960-SPKM.28.8.A
R1	1	1K Î© Resistor A-2200 66-CMF1/41001FLFTR
R2	1	22K Î© Resistor A-2284 603-MFR-25FRF52-22K
R3	2	560 Î© Resistor A-2282 603-MFR-25FTE52-560R
RV1, RV2	2	B500 KÎ© Potentiometer A-1849 317-3090F-500K
RV3	1	B 1 MÎ© Potentiometer A-1882 652-PTV09A4020FB105
U1, U2	2	TLC555CP Single LinCMOS Timer, 555 compatible, PDIP-8 NOT Listed 595-TLC555CP
NULL	1	Breadboard Breadboard A-2372 932-MIKROE-1097
NULL	1	Jumper Wires Jumper Wires A-6152 854-ZW-MM-10
NULL	1	Clips Alligator Clips (Connect to speaker) A-6574 548-287 or 854-CA-M-20

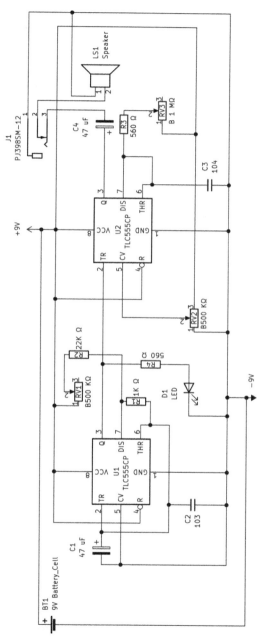

"Schematics" by BENT NOISE

FRONT - NO PARTS

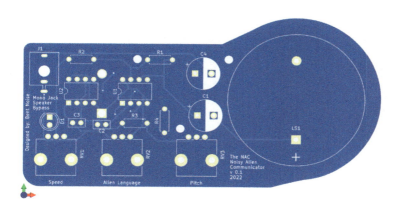

FRONT - FINISHED

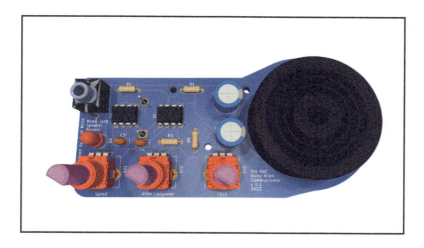

BACK - NO PARTS

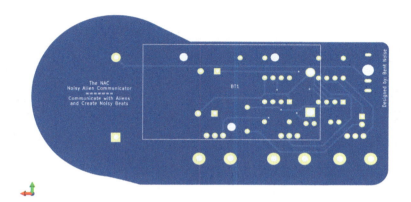

BACK - FINISHED

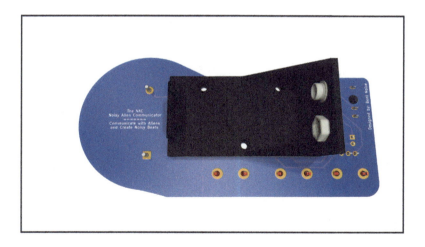

NOISY ALIEN COMMMUNICATOR

ASSEMBLY REQUIRED. SEND OUT HARSH FREQUENCIES AND COMMUNICATE WITH THE UNIVERSE. MAYBE SOME ALIENS WILL REPLY, OR DOGS WILL BARK.

EITHER WAY YOU WILL BE ABLE TO STAR IN YOUR OWN ADVENTURE.

- SQUARE WAVES
- OSCILLATE
- PITCH AND TONE

DEMONSTRATION VIDEO: HTTPS://YOUTU.BE/LBITBIH6RXA
VENDOR OPTIONS: taydaelectronics.com   mouser.com
ADDITIONAL PARTS VENDORS: jameco.com   digikey.com

BREAD BOARD

Contents

PART I: NOISY ALIEN COMMUNICATOR

Sending the Wrong Message
by Bertram Montiekowicz 19
Ground Lightning
by Matt Bitonti 33
The Search for Intelligent Life
by Bertram Montiekowicz 45
The Stripper Story
by Jackrabbit 63
Breach Horizon
by Paradox M. Pollack 79

PART II: THE VISIBLE SPECTRUM

A Walk Through Greenpoint
by Jackrabbit 101
Proof Through the Night
by Paradox M. Pollack 119
The Jazz
by Matt Bitonti 147
A Landfill Adventurer's Guide
by Robert V. Kilroy 159
The Human Virus
by Bertram Montiekowicz 189

PART I: NOISY ALIEN COMMUNICATOR

Sending the Wrong Message

by Bertram Montiekowicz

For Melvin Doppler, just another normal day: he worked about a half hour and hoped to spend the next eight immersed in his favorite virtual reality experience. Like most married men, he had started to look like his wife, and the mandibles on their rostrums were almost identical. They had fallen into the regular routine any husband and wife might feel after two hundred and fifty years of marriage.

Then, his wife screamed, "Pick up the goddamned phone!"

"You pick up the goddamned phone!"

"I'm watching something!"

"You don't think I'm watching something!"

"It's an important part!"

"Oh, goddammit!" Melvin disconnected from his screen but the phone wasn't ringing anymore. After a pregnant pause he added one last shout. "What was the point?"

"Well who was it?"

He looked at the display. "Unknown."

"Unknown? What the hell does that mean?"

It rang again. Melvin picked it up. "Hello." Hearing nothing he pressed the phone deeper into the moist listening hole astride his muscular head appendage. "Hello? Hello?" He hung up.

His wife could barely contain her temper. "Who the hell was it?"

"No answer, just static."

"Static?" She slithered into the doorway. "I thought they got rid of that?"

"Hmm."

"You should call the police."

"The police!"

"Yeah, what if it's some creep."

Melvin picked up the phone and pressed one button.

A robot said, "You have called the police! Please state your emergency or, hang up."

"I need to see an officer right now."

"Officer arriving in five, four, three . . . ."

***

Officer Lucy Sheridan thought it was just going to be another normal day. She got a good night's sleep, ate a healthy breakfast, and when she arrived in her uniform everyone greeted her cordially. She stepped into the teleportation pod and watched the call screen for emergencies.

A cat had been safely removed from a sludge processing gutter, but the officer had been scratched and rushed to the hospital for fear of infection. Across town an old lady pushing a baby carriage with three dogs on a leash was attempting to cross a busy street, and so traffic had to be redirected to a higher elevation. Then the Doppler call.

Each residence had a teleportation pad outside their front door. The Dopplers seemed like normal people, the steel casing on their walkway shined red, showing recent polish, the garden arrayed to regulation. As Officer Sheridan made her initial conclusions the door to the residence flew open, and there stood Helen Doppler.

"It's about time you got here!"

Helen morphed aside as Officer Sheridan slid through the doorway and climbed onto the couch. With one of her skin flaps Lucy pulled a mint from the bowl, and as she dropped it into her eating mouth, her speaking mouth asked, "Why did you call the police?"

Melvin Doppler burst into the room, tightening his robe. "Office Sheridan."

The mint dissolved with a burst of flavor. "I was just asking your wife...."

Helen said, "We're getting crank called."

"Crank called?"

Melvin said, "Yes, twice. I'm busy, you know?"

Officer Sheridan noticed another bowl on the table that looked like pills. "What are these?"

He said, "Feel good."

Sheridan ingested a flapful and sat back on the couch. "So what exactly do you want the police to do about it?"

Helen knew. "Find out who it is!"

Sheridan smiled. "You know we can't access the System."

Melvin lost his temper. "We have a right to know who is calling our own goddamned phone!"

Sheridan showed him a set of empty flaps. "Whoa, whoa, whoa, let's start at the beginning. Who did the phone say was calling?"

Helen said, "It said Unknown. What does that even mean?"

Lucy lost her good humor, wishing she hadn't swallowed so many pills. She slid onto the floor. "Let's go."

Melvin grabbed a flapful of pills for himself and choked them down with an injection of H_2O from a hose that hung from the ceiling. "I'm ready."

Detective Agnes Thoreau had a fast paced normal day. Most of her calls were of a financial nature, stopping price manipulators on the derivative markets, disrupting roving off-planet tax shelters, revealing data forgeries. She had a murder once. So when Officer Sheridan and the Dopplers arrived outside her office she immediately froze her programs and led the three of them to the witness area, where their testimony could be preserved.

After recording the complaint Thoreau dissected the video and audio evidence as the Dopplers watched. Then she uploaded the most pertinent details into a file that was almost immediately accessed and put under review as they waited. Lucy tried to speak as little as possible as she knew the detective could hear the vast quantity of pills in her voice.

Thoreau didn't have time to notice. She focused on reassuring the Dopplers, who were visibly shaken. "Don't worry, we'll find out who is behind this in a matter of moments. You understand we have to be careful who accesses the System and for what reason. It's not that we don't trust Officer Sheridan or anyone else to access the System, but by controlling the access, we can be sure who altered the data, and this is how we prevent misinformation. Misinformation is very dangerous, you understand. So that's the way it is. We know who called you, but you don't; it doesn't seem fair, does it?"

"You're damn right it doesn't!" Melvin screamed. The pills had kicked in but once he got going it was hard to stop.

Helen held a different tone as she felt they were close to resolution. "What will the punishment be?"

Thoreau's guard came up and she spread across the chair, choosing her next words carefully. "Let's not get ahead of ourselves."

Melvin shifted his weight forward so he could loom larger, standing taller than he had a moment ago. "What's taking so long?"

***

System Administrator Jeff Jenkins' normal day involved a two-hour shift, mostly approving routing requests into, out of and through the System. Indeed the checks and authorizations he provided were not to the letter of the law, and everybody up and down the chain understood government standards were more like guideposts, and if any litigation ensued, the ultimate purpose behind these layers of processing would come to the fore, as everyone would want to know who had checked which box when.

Jenkins jumped on the request from Thoreau as he had a great deal of respect for her, and everyone thought highly of her work ethic. 'Who just called me'-type requests were routine, usually. Jenkins had never seen an Unknown Caller. He took a moment to search through The Book, where he learned an Unknown designation could only come from an offworld source outside the Empire with which no one has ever had any previous contact.

A bead of sweat appeared on Jenkins' uppermost upper lip; he was going to have to talk to his boss.

* * *

Elizabeth Masterinow enjoyed a normal day with a tremendous amount of quiet. Over her five hundred and twenty years of life, nearly a century had been spent managing System Access Authorization. The workflows were so dynamic no one ever needed to call. So when Jenkins appeared on her screen, Elizabeth could not help but morph up.

"What is it?"

Jenkins tried to keep his cool. "Ah, um, Helen and Melvin Doppler, you may not know them, they live in Mulch Gulley, they entered a complaint about a crank call, apparently they both had to drop out of their Level-up and um, now they have to find a new Guild, so they're pretty pissed, but the reason I called you is, I mean, you're not going to believe it but, the crank call came from another galaxy."

"Another galaxy!" most of Director Masterinow's eyeballs protruded from her lower forehead. Her two hearts fell out of synchrony. "Which one?"

"The Milky Way."

Masterinow struggled to catch her breath. "I thought there was no intelligent life in the Milky Way."

"It's true, we've never gotten anything from them before."

Masterinow lost the strength necessary to hold her head appendage stable. "This is going to have to go all the way up to Planetary Security. Let Thoreau know we're working on it, she's probably got her hands full." Jenkins completed the routing request and within minutes Director Masterinow found herself being raced off to the hospital, and the prognosis was not good.

***

A normal day for Agent Sally Prendergrast of Planetary Security would be spent in the lower atmosphere redirecting meteors, watching the screen mostly but sometimes driving the drone herself. The time passed quickly. Rarely did she concern herself with the surface, but obviously, it remained her priority.

The Masterinow Upload, her last, had struck a chord among the staff at Planetary Security, leaving the agents edgy and eager for payback. Sally was happy to get the high-profile assignment.

Sally appeared in the Doppler's doorway alongside the married couple as they returned home from the police station. Officer Sheridan and Detective Thoreau accompanied the Dopplers, eager to complete their forms and curious about who might ultimately review them. By then they all knew Masterinow probably wouldn't last the day, lending the meeting an air of solemnity. The small group continued to share introductions and condolences until the front door opened. There stood little Alvin Doppler, still in his front diaper; he was only 21.

Helen could not contain her fury. "Why aren't you in front of your screen?"

Melvin, blissfully high, laughed, and this seemed to set Helen off, as she only took pills to sleep. She slid forward, one of her skin flaps hardened as if to smack the child, but the boy said, "I'm sorry Momma but the phone won't stop ringing." They all turned an eye towards each other. Then they heard it themselves, echoing through the foyer. The wiry hairs on Detective Thoreau's pinky stood on end.

Agent Prendergast said, "I'm going to answer it!"

"No!" Helen almost screamed. She led the way towards the phone and the others silently followed. The elder Doppler pressed the phone to her biggest ear. "Hello. Hello. Hello!"

Melvin asked, "Well?"

"Nothing." She hung up.

Sally said, "Let me in there."

Helen stepped away but her husband wanted a closer look. Sheridan and Thoreau found a place on the couch, eagerly sampling the mints and pills.

The equipment Agent Prendergast brought connected to the Doppler's phone, and within seconds the data began accumulating. To satisfy everyone's curiosity Sally commandeered the main screen in the Doppler's living room. Helen found the best seat, forcing Sheridan to slide to the edge of the couch. Melvin remained erect, his talking mouth twisted in a sick grin while his eating mouth gaped. With the connections in place, Sally also took a comfortable seat.

She said, "Let's zoom in on where the signal is coming from. Our Milky Way maps are pretty good. It's crazy to think this call originated eleven million trillion miles away. There we go, we're locked in."

The screen showed a planet, four thousand mile radius, less than a hundred million miles from a G-type main sequence star. The molten core provided a magnetosphere that blocked the deadly radiation while allowing heat and preserving an atmosphere. The planet had one smooth moon, bright blue seas, lush green land and white fluffy clouds.

Sally said, "It's going to take at least ten minutes to download these radiowaves, they've been shooting them out for over a hundred years. Seems like a lot of nonsense. Wait, this is good, they have their data gathered in central locations, just a couple companies are sitting on these treasure troves. Here's the number, the whole planet only has a hundred and seventy five zettabytes total. This won't take long. No real security. The databots are in there now. While we're waiting, let's see how close we can get with the live camera." With one flap on the dial, Sally brought them closer to the world. "Wow look at that, cities and roads, bridges and satellites. They've got quite a little civilization going here!"

Melvin pointed at the screen. "There's one. They're so funny looking! They look like lollipops."

Helen could not contain her emotions. "But why are they calling me?"

Detective Thoreau said, "That's a good question."

Lucy, floating in fluffy clouds herself, said, "I have a guess . . . I think they're trying to feel us out, to see what we'll do, how we'll react."

Thoreau chewed on the idea for a long moment before popping another pill. "You may be right."

Sally said, "Ok, here's the first batch of data. Well, there you go, say no more, they tax their people. That tells you all you need to know. Everybody has to pay, wait, not everybody. They employ a complicated system that allows the rich to avoid paying their fair share. Looks to me like a bifurcated society. The rich nations tax their people and use the money to make weapons of war, which they use to threaten each other. One nation claims to be a global superpower. Says here they waste a hundred billion pounds of food every year while seven hundred million starve. For H2O the average superpower family wastes about 200 gallons a week while a billion of their fellow creatures have no access to clean drinkable."

To break the tense silence, Sheridan said, "They sound like monsters!"

Thoreau added, "This feels like a caustic form of provocation. The audacity; I guess they think we'll be afraid, I guess they think if they brandish their weapons of war we will be overawed, and they can turn us into their next colony, and before you know it, we'll be the ones starving and dying of thirst."

Then the phone rang again. Melvin slid backwards as the police officers morphed up in unison.

Sally said, "Now that we're locked in maybe we'll get better reception."

Helen used her shortest flap to pick up the phone, the others were shaking so badly. "Hello?"

A voice could be heard, originating in another galaxy, and now amplified through the audio visual equipment connected to the screen in the Doppler's living room. The robot translators identified the language as English but could not render any meaning, even after later study. The voice said, "Imagine if this actually worked, ahuh."

The phone slipped from Helen's grip and would have shattered had Lucy not caught it with her toes. Melvin fainted into a broad pool and had to be squeegeed from the room by Sheridan and Thoreau. Most of Prendergrast's eyes were stony, as she knew this needed to be on the President's desk, ASAP. Her tell-tale third eye shifted nervously, coated in slimy tear.

* * *

President Carol Shaw never had a normal day. Her term lasted nearly five years, over which her approval rating dropped below 80% only once, mostly, she claimed, because of misrepresentations about her education proposals. The drop in approval rating forced an immediate election, but when no challenger emerged to run against her, Shaw returned to favorable status. She gave an impassioned speech about her dedication to everyone's prosperity, and how as President she would always be there for her people, especially those who viewed her most unfavorably.

No one really wanted to be President and few had lasted as long as Carol Shaw. Her forebears had decided long ago that transparent government works best. Anyone on the planet could switch their screen and see exactly where the President was, who they were with, listen to what they were talking about, at any time of the day. Some of Shaw's most viral moments were from when she slept, as she often spoke incoherently and one time shouted "Goal," after which her rear trunk grew semi-erect, an image that had been successfully deployed countless times as a motivation meme.

In the moments after the call arrived from Planetary Security, the President's viewership numbers spiked, alerting everyone to switch screens. The crank calling crisis had all the drama, killing Director Masterinow, victimizing the Dopplers with lost Guild status and measurable emotional pain, the roles played by hard working government officials up and down the chain of command. Online game play dipped. At the peak, 93.6% of the population was watching the President, breaking the record of 85.7% held by juggling escape artist Dr. Fink during his Fire in the Sky special.

* * *

Back at the Dopplers, the phone rang again. Prendergrast sounded grave. "It's them."

From her chair in the capital city, Shaw gave the order, "Answer it."

Helen again grabbed the phone, this time with two flaps. "Hello? Hello!"

A different voice speaking English came through, translated as, "Stop Bogarting." The databots sifted through the available data but the meaning of the statement could not immediately be determined, as counter-culture sources were dismissed. "Stop" they understood to be an order, the entire population felt it, but for the second word there were numerous audio records but few written explanations. Stop what? What had the aliens ordered them to do? Bogart referred to a person, an actor who played the tough guy role in movies. The System came to its conclusion, sharing it with the world as the President watched: the aliens had ordered them to stop acting like a tough guy.

Network traffic spiked as everyone reached out to comfort loved ones and friends. Shaw clamped down on both jaws before facing camera one. "Our world has been invaded by a brutal primitive people. We must choose the appropriate response. I'm preparing a poll now." Seven flaps moved feverishly.

"Option 1, ignore and block; now that we know about this menace, we can simply change the channel so to speak. Option 2, send a death ray to destroy this world before these provocations get any worse. The way these creatures treat the weakest among them shows what they will do to us and anyone who looks different; you'd have to say we'd be doing the universe a big favor. Or Option 3, and this one intrigues me. We can study this world and learn everything we can, they have H_2O, maybe we can breathe their air? Then we simply remove the current population, take their place; seems like a nice enough planet, I like what I see so far. I trust you will make the right decision. The poll is up, and will close in one hour. Now get back out there and start shopping."

* * *

In the end, the people wanted to send Dave Moore to find out what was happening. Dave Moore had no official title, no regular day. He had been off-world before but never in such dangerous circumstances. His destination on earth had more firearms per capita than most states, almost two per person. Two shotguns were packed in the back of the garage where the crank call emerged, but it seemed none of the occupants knew they were there.

Hardly the sort of reassuring prep talk Moore had come to expect from his team. On an average day, over three hundred people are shot; he wasn't going to be one of them. The nearby city had two-hundred and fifty shootings in the last lunar cycle. If the perpetrators fled in that direction, Moore was not going to pursue. Despite the prevalence of firearms, his real risk came from other weapons, vehicles, bludgeoning, ropes, and knives. One of the perpetrators had a small razor-like blade on the end of a metal stick. If statistics held, Moore's attacker would be someone he had come to know or someone paid with tax money to protect the peace.

Not much time to prepare. After many hours the crank callers were breaking up, heading in different directions, making any contact with the perpetrators more challenging. Based on their research, once earthlings split up, each would claim a different version of events, refusing to change their story, despite audio or visual evidence.

Confronting these earthlings would present a series of challenges Moore had prepared for his entire life.

He made his way into a secure location, one of their cars. After quietly setting it directly in front of the garage doors, Moore pooled into all four seats. If you looked carefully, you could see his sensory organs peeking through mirrors and windows.

When the garage door flew up, Moore used a tool to send a burst of blinding energy into the car's headlights, and the perpetrators were suitably cowed.

Moore eyed them as he tried to put together the situation.

These were not adult earthlings, not mature certainly. It seemed their time in the garage involved playing a role-playing game. Crank calling the Dopplers was not the primary reason they had gotten together. One of them had begun dabbling with electrical engineering, ordinary enough, but in the course of his study, had inadvertently developed a tool capable of sending a message across the universe. Now they assumed they were busted for combusting a dried plant.

The team had prepared a few statements for Moore to project in English

"What are you doing?"

They had their hands raised in surrender. Moore counted seven in all, some with tears in their eyes. At least three were speaking, but there was no way to make sense of it. After preparing to face the array of weapons the earthlings had amassed, Moore remembered one key statistic: often the wounds would be self-inflicted.

Their feeble words made Moore sick to his stomachs. Pleading for mercy, to avoid harsh consequences, imprisoned alongside the worst their society could muster. These young earth men were so afraid, how could people live in abject fear, all because they wanted to smoke a weed and imagine they had great strength and charisma?

Moore made his decision. If he continued with his interrogation, they might see his form, which would cause more problems than just terminating the entire mission. The last thing he heard as he left the scene was, "Dude, what was that?" and "I thought you parked over there?"

Returned to the planet of his birth, Moore saw President Shaw looming.

"Back so soon?"

Moore began removing the careful weave of elements and filaments protecting his frame. "It's a non-starter."

"What do you mean?"

"Just kids, goofing around, nothing the universe needs to be concerned with. This Earth, it's nothing new. How many times have we seen it? People developing technologies far superior to their wisdom, surpassing their maturity of how to best employ it. I doubt we'll be hearing from those earthlings again. They'll never make it all the way out here in any case. They're too much of a risk to themselves."

The president looked at her advisors and turned to Camera 1.

"Well, what do you think of that? Is that enough for you? Should people be able to do whatever they want in this universe, or should we feel the pain of these poor earthlings if they seem unable to feel for themselves? If they are powerless to get fair treatment, is it our duty to ignore their plight? One might argue this message reached us for a reason. I'd love to hear what you think. Look for a new poll, the countdown is on. I trust you'll make the right decision."

Ground Lightning

by Matt Bitonti

The alien's vision was obscured: only brown specks of crumbly soil around him. He gasped, finding air that smelled like freshly cut grass. He climbed over the dirt, and the first thing he saw was an oblong spheroid. It was striped, dimpled, and sat perched atop the manicured university quad grass. From his perspective, a tenth of the size of a wood mouse, the blades of grass were tree-sized stilts, holding up an enormous boulder. The shadow it cast made the alien almost invisible. Looking up against the stars and the crescent moon, the word on the stone seemed larger than life.

GILBERT. He liked how it sounded. So he took it for a name.

Size, of course, was a matter of perspective. Gilbert was miniature compared to the human footprints in the grass. As he crawled away from what he would later learn was a rugby ball, his alien figure found DNA. It was a wayward skin flake from an adult male who lost it playing something called "Ultimate Frisbee." It wasn't perfect, but he would use it to create his vehicle.

He looked around and confirmed he was alone. An unknown instinct deep within his skull told him to keep his true nature secret. It was one of his prime directives. The other was to help creatures, great and small, sentient or not, as many as possible before returning to his home planet.

Humanity had many words for Gilbert's kind: the Chinese called them mogwai. The Europeans called them fairies, elves, and nymphs. The most accurate term for his anatomy was probably homunculus. He was a tiny being, about to control a much bigger one. Religion called them angels, sometimes adding the modifier guardian. He couldn't fly, but it was an apt description of his job.

Technically, he was a gardener unit, sent across the stars encased in rock. His job was to tend the garden of intelligent life. He flew, asleep for eons, entombed against the void of space. Like many of his kind, he fell through the sky and lay frozen in the mud until the exact tones rang out. The discordant pitches, historically emitted from the larynx of a dying creature or a broken musical instrument, heralded the start of his life.

His ears perked: there it was again: a wailing keen, seeming random but an acutely fine pattern. The noise must have come from nearby. The brick buildings covered in crawling ivy looked primitive but sturdy. An instinct told Gilbert the noise came from the third floor, the corner dorm facing west. He would go to that location and assist that individual. Along the way, he would help more, as many as he could. It wasn't a choice. He was compelled.

***

Help, of course, was a matter of perspective. Gilbert knew that his performance would be evaluated by the home planet when he was called to harvest. His goal was not just to assist life but to hurt as little of it in the process—the butterfly effect and all that. Wiping humanity clean with an apocalypse to save the whales wouldn't win him any points with the higher-ups. He had to tread lightly if he wanted any chance at re-assignment.

Gilbert dove under the dirt again. The source of the tone would have to wait another day. Gilbert could feel his body weaken, preparing for the change, extracting the minerals from the soil. He needed these elements to disguise himself in the form of one of these humans.

While Gilbert was transforming, he processed the archives of the gardeners, those who came before him to this local corner of the galaxy. Besides finding out what worked before, he didn't want to repeat the mistakes of history. He had hours to wait inside the cocoon, but the archives were thorough and gave him plenty of reading material.

When Gilbert determined his human form was complete, he felt great joy. He couldn't wait to get started. Unable to control his emotions, Gilbert popped out of the ground head-first, expelled upward like bread from a toaster. In mid-air, he realized that he had overshot this planet's physics. That was how Gilbert found himself nude and hanging from a massive pine tree branch.

From his height, Earth looked bucolic. The early morning dew had not yet evaporated from the springtime quad. The dark paths were sparsely populated, convenient given his current state. Still, he saw a shorter human, a female who had stopped on the pathways to gawk. She calmly sipped her hot drink and shouted to Gilbert.

"Hey up there, nature boy! Do you need help? Or are you just part of some freaky art installation?"

Gilbert's command of language was weak, but he understood the word "art." It was one of the main methods used by previous agents to enlighten this primitive species. DaVinci, Dali, Rothko were a few of the names his fellow gardeners had taken. Art could spread enlightenment. If this person knew art, could take him to the art, perhaps he could make progress with his mission. Besides, his arms grew sore and sticky with pine sap, so he let go and plunged into a mulched area of twigs and grass clippings. The vegetation clung to his naked frame, giving him the look of some kind of rugged survivalist.

"Yes," he said, establishing his posture. "Where is art?"

The young woman smirked with realization. "The accent, of course. You must be the new Figure Drawing model the Professor talked up. The foreign exchange student. I'm going there, too." Gilbert looked at her dumbly. The student sighed. "Follow me, Adonis."

"Not Adonis. I am Gilbert."

"Well, Gilbert, I'm Ronnie. I get that you're confident and all, but aren't you supposed to have like a robe or something?"

Gilbert only shrugged. Ronnie had a stressed look on her face that went beyond his lack of wardrobe. The lines in her forehead spoke volumes. She was like a seedling, leaning to the wrong side or perhaps beset by weeds. But humans weren't plants. An investigation was required to determine their problems.

Gilbert reached out his aura and found the wifi. Then he used the same atmosphere to invisibly search her possessions. The magnetic stripe of a bank card led to an account with only 36 dollars in it. Other cards carried negative amounts, debt that she owed. Reaching further, he found messages on a primitive communication device between Veronica (her full name) and her family. Her mother needed expensive medication and surgeries. But Ronnie couldn't help. Just study, her mother texted. You've abandoned the family, her father texted. It all broke Gilbert's heart.

Gilbert frowned. This lack of money was causing her stress. The fix was simple enough. He interacted with the magnetic strips and the wifi and merely moved some decimal points. She no longer had debt. In fact, these companies now owed her money. Gilbert wanted to say something, but he also loved surprises.

As Gilbert boosted Ronnie's credit score, they walked silently toward a modernist brick building with what looked like a hole punched in the middle of it. Ronnie swiped a white laminated card on the door to the Visual Art Center and held the glass door open. Gilbert tracked dirt footprints over its waxed wooden floors. She led Gilbert up the stairs to the art studio on the third floor, already filled with eager students.

"Look who I found, just hanging around."

The Professor, disheveled and manic, gave Gilbert a strange look, making a note of his skin sticky with pine sap and the fragments of mulch tangled in his hair. "Excellent. Primal." He wasted no time pushing Gilbert up on the platform. "I'm glad you were able to make it. You sounded pretty sick over text." Gilbert said nothing but made a mental note to heal that foreign exchange student, should they cross paths.

"Class, this is... I'm sorry, what was your name again?"

"Gilbert."

"Class, this is Gil. And as you can see, he is the pinnacle of the idealized human form. Michaelangelo's 'David' has nothing on Mister Gilbert here."

The students made no moves, merely bathing in Gilbert's aura. As Gilbert learned from the documentation, mesmerizing the locals was a common danger. Thankfully the Professor wasn't so easily distracted.

"What are you waiting for? Draw!"

The room burst into a flurry of motion, and Gilbert pushed out his abilities toward the group. The students found it easier than ever. Pencils flew. Without exception, these sketches would be the best session of the term: being in Gilbert's presence forced every last ounce of artistic skill out of the group.

Everyone was happy, engaged in an elevated flow state, except the Professor. Gilbert reached into his mind and found it riddled with chemical addiction. Beyond the top layer of buzzy caffeine, this person had a secret opioid habit and simply could not face the withdrawal. While Gilbert posed, he led the Professor to lay his head down on his desk and fall asleep. Gilbert altered his brain chemistry through the air. It was child's play. The Professor simply wouldn't crave those little round devils when he awoke.

The rising sun tracked up the glass while the class was in a fugue state of concentration. Then, Gilbert moved. It was the tone again, the one that awakened him in the dirt. It emitted from the same third-floor window, and it compelled him to move, to find the source, but he had to extract himself from the current situation.

Gilbert sent a mental signal to the Professor, who picked his head up. "Huh. I must have dozed off there." He wandered around the easels, yawning. He paused, dumbstruck by skills he didn't know his students possessed.

"Well then, Gilbert, it appears you have inspired everyone today to new heights. Very good. Very good, indeed. Class dismissed."

The students left, and Gilbert too began to walk out, but the Professor stopped him and pointed him toward a closet filled with college merch.

"Here, Gilbert. Clothe yourself. You made an impressive entrance, but I don't want to be blamed when you scandalize the entire campus." Gilbert didn't understand, but the idea he would cause a problem made him sad. He slowly put on a tracksuit, white with black trim. He zipped up, and over his breast, the gleaming white head of a polar bear floated.

"Puritanism, I know. It's a real bummer." The Professor's eye's lingered on Gilbert's bare feet, but Gilbert only smiled. "Are you hungry?" The Professor asked. "I'm starving all of a sudden."

Gilbert evaluated his human container, and he discovered that, in fact, he was starving. The energy required to create his human carrier and work miracles around campus was extreme. He did need to recharge his batteries. Gilbert then understood the worth of this Professor, sort of a human gardener of his own - just with cruder tools.

Gilbert's bare feet fell in step with the Professors' penny loafers. They walked through the quad, making a straight shot east. They walked next to an elegant gray church and across a grassy roundabout. "I apologize for walking so fast," the Professor said. "But I haven't felt this spry in years - or as hungry." As the Professor held the door open, a humid cloud of scent enveloped Gilbert's face. He didn't know exactly what it was, but his human stomach audibly gurgled with desire.

"You really did a fantastic job this morning," the Professor noted as he fished out his laminated key card. It had been hanging around his neck on a Polar Bear lanyard under his sweater. "So, this is on me."

The Professor swiped his card twice, a stunning show of generosity by the alien's standards. In return, Gilbert made sure to replace the units digitally. In fact, he added a few thousand extra "Polar Points" to be sure, not just for the Professor but for everyone within range. Indeed, every garden needed nutrients. Gilbert hoped this feeding facility had the supply to handle the influx of currency.

As he rounded the corner and saw the feast presented before him, Gilbert put that fear to the side. Dishes of every color and consistency greeted him, and he merely stood there, spoiled for choice. This garden had nutrients to spare.

The Professor approached Gilbert and leaned in with advice. "If I were a scientist, I'd tell you to go for the protein, maybe some high fiber options. But as an artist, I have the luxury of starting my day in reverse." He led Gilbert to a frosted metal cart with tins of various colored sludges. The toppers stood nearby: impossibly red cherries, cans of whipped cream, and glossy decorations, all in tiny glass bowls with miniature serving spoons.

"This, my foreign friend, is the 'Make-Your-Own-Sundae' bar. And it's as close to heaven as some of us are ever gonna get."

The Professor (vanilla, crushed Oreos, and strawberries) and Gilbert (rocky road with the works) sat down in a booth with their sundaes. Gilbert poked it gingerly and followed the Professor's lead. Within an instant, Gilbert devoured the creamy treat. Too fast, as the stabbing pains in his forehead informed him. The Professor only laughed. The alien was sure his time on the planet had come to an end, but a few seconds later, Gilbert was completely normal again, no worse for wear. He stood up from the booth, grabbed a clean tray, and gathered a little of everything the cafeteria had to offer.

The buffet area was full of busy students crisscrossing his path without noticing. Gilbert reached out: Brooke had ignorant opinions about some of her fellow students. Ethan didn't know the value of hard work. Emma had the precursors to blood cancer. Easy fixes, all changed with a blink of Gilbert's eye.

Gilbert looked up at two students arguing outside. Their tone had grown angry. Then the smaller one slapped the bigger one across the face. And the bigger one grabbed the smaller one with both hands. They both had tears in their eyes. Gilbert put down his tray and ran outside, and pushed his way through the crowd that had started to form.

"How could you, Madison? How could you do this?"

The male was visibly distraught and undoubtedly capable of violence. Previous gardeners described this exact encounter type in the archives. Interference in domestic disputes rarely went well. Still, Gilbert wanted to try.

Gilbert put his hand on the man's shoulder. "Easy there, friend. Maybe you should take a breath and calm down."

"Don't you touch me!" The male reached back, gathered a fist, and threw a wild haymaker toward Gilbert. The gardener stepped aside, followed the man's punch all around, and wrapped the man in his own arm like a scarf. Onlookers saw a rear choke. Barely touching him, Gilbert instantly put him to sleep.

"What did you do! Leave him alone!" Madison lunged through her tears with balled-up fists. Gilbert caught her too by the scruff of the neck and put her to sleep. The crowd muttered. Gilbert held two humans, one in each hand around the back of the neck. Their bodies hung limp like sleeping kittens. This wasn't good.

He placed them on the ground and considered wiping everyone's memory of the incident, as the risk of unintended consequences was far too high. Over his shoulder, two burly campus officers approached. His secrecy instinct kicked in hard. Instead of trying to explain, he ran away, his polyester tracksuit rippling in the breeze. Gilbert lept out an open window, tore through a copse of trees and dropped, hiding in the shadows. The soil was always his friend; the instinct came from deep within. Once the scene cleared, he sprinted across the quad toward where he last heard the tone.

* * *

The door was locked, so Gilbert waited again in the mud. This time he hid underneath short hedges, watching students filter in and out of the brick building. Gilbert crept closer to the opening and, after one substantial student swung it wide, slipped his hand into the door before the hydraulics closed completely. His human container took damage, but Gilbert made no noise.

The tone played out again, so Gilbert bounded up the stairs. His jumpsuit, formerly white and shiny, now was dull with brown stains. He went up the stairs and heard music on the third-floor landing. He recognized it in the archives from one of his fellow gardeners: Prince, or the Artist Formerly Known as Prince. Gilbert chuckled at the quantum superposition, how the same being could be known as both. That was a good gardener joke. Elvis, Bowie, Jimi, Janis, and Kurt were other gardeners in the archives who picked music as their weapon of choice. Many had come and gone, their time on this planet short.

The tone warbled again. It came from the door at the end of the hallway.

Prince was a legendary gardener, as was Leonardo DiVinci. But Gilbert wasn't a musician, and he wasn't much of an artist, despite his appearance in Figure Drawing. Maybe he was a muse?

As he walked down the hallway toward the tone, it became clear to Gilbert what gardener archetype he was falling into: the messiah. Old-school, in-person miracles, these were his true nature. Gilbert stopped in front of the door and sighed before he knocked. To be a messiah was one of the noblest specialties a gardener could choose. You helped, healed, and fed many. But they had the shortest lives of all. And it always ended in the same way: with violent self-sacrifice.

Gilbert knocked, and a skinny brown-haired boy opened the door.

"Yeah?"

"You called me."

The boy twitched with a flicker of recognition. "I didn't call anyone." Gilbert smiled and pointed over the boy's shoulder toward the circuit board.

The boy's desk was immaculately organized, with wires, motors, and other engineering parts categorized in clear plastic drawers. But the circuit board on the desk that emitted the tone was a snarl of circuitry connected to a joystick. Above the setup, a video hung, paused. "How to make the NAC: Noisy Alien Communicator," the clip was titled. Submitted by a user named "Bent Noise." Gilbert made a mental note. Someone was teaching these primitives how to make NACs, and it could only be a leak from the home office.

The boy smiled and welcomed Gilbert inside. "I can't believe that worked." He held out a fist. "I'm Lucas."

"Gilbert," the alien replied, bumping Lucas's knuckles. These hairless primates and their charming little habits were starting to grow on him.

"You're an alien, huh?"

Gilbert only shrugged.

"Well, I'm going to assume you are because I need your help. That's why I built that whiney hunk of junk and even hunted down a part from 1976 to do it. That's before my dad was born, ya know? Because I knew it was real. I just knew." Gilbert did his best to look receptive, despite not understanding. The boy talked too fast.

Lucas took a deep breath. "The thing is, Gilbert, my brain is different than everyone else's. They say I should use the word neuro-atypical, but that's just a fancy way to say I'm different. And probably dumb. They give me pills and extra time for tests, but it's never enough time." Lucas sat down, deflated. "And I'm all alone over here. No one understands my differences, and I can't take it anymore. You're an all-powerful alien, so you fix this." He pointed at his temple. His tears welled. "I just want to find love and be normal. That won't happen the way things are now. So I need you to fix my brain, Gilbert. Please."

Gilbert nodded, and the boy closed his eyes. He reached out to examine the brain of this poor little seedling. The alien hated to see anyone in pain and loved making quick fixes. But as Gilbert delved into Lucas' mind, he found a well of almost infinitely vast intelligence. The deeper he looked, the more it grew, spiraling into itself over and over like a fractal. This Lucas told the truth: the boy had a severe learning disability. But he also possessed possibly the most incredible human brain since Albert Einstein. It would be a sin to tamper with a brain of this magnitude.

Einstein was not a gardener, for the record. But one of the patent clerks who worked next to Einstein was. That gardener recorded his workmate's potential and Einstein's similarly odd learning disabilities in the archives. Gardeners ask the flowers to bloom, but no one can force them.

The boy opened his eyes. "Did you do it? I don't feel any different."

"I'm sorry," Gilbert said, shaking his head. "I can't."

"What do you mean, you can't? You're an alien. That's your job."

"Lucas, your brain is extraordinary." Gilbert tried to explain. "Perhaps one in a billion. Maybe even rarer than that. You could be one of history's great minds. It would go against my directives to interfere."

There were tears in the boy's eyes. "I don't believe you. You're not an alien. That's the same believe-in-yourself lies everyone's been feeding me my whole life. I don't want to be special."

Gilbert saw a cloud forming over the boy's aura, the self-hatred that often ended in suicide. If Lucas did make that mistake, it could have global, even galaxy-wide, consequences.

"You are special, Lucas. You have to believe me," Gilbert pleaded, but it was clear his words weren't enough to restore Lucas' faith in life. This seedling wanted deeds, proof.

Outside, storm clouds gathered over the quad. They were far off but moving quickly over the spring wind. Gilbert sighed because he knew what he had to do.

"Fine, you don't have to believe me," Gilbert said. "But I want you to look out that window and keep an open mind when you do." Gilbert walked calmly out of the room and into the hallway. From the stairwell, he heard more music, this time a gardener who called herself Dolores and sang with the Cranberries. Salvation is free, the singer cried out. Salvation is free.

Gilbert walked outside, and the storm clouds gathered, dimming the skies. He stood on the grass and looked back at the dorm. He had to make sure Lucas was watching. The boy's head was there, peering skeptically through the transparent pane. Gilbert felt relief. He wouldn't be able to perform this miracle twice.

The wind roared, and peels of thunder echoed off the brick buildings. The sky darkened unnaturally, almost as if a mighty asteroid were bearing down on the campus. Gilbert kept eye contact with Lucas. The alien smiled and pointed upward. The skies opened up with rain, fat heavy drops that cracked against the hard pavement when it hit.

Lucas watched as Gilbert triggered his harvest sequence. It was a short existence, but he hoped he did enough to keep his job. A white orb manifested over Gilbert's head, rotating and extending tendrils of lightning around the container Gilbert built. One blinding flash and the container vaporized. Gilbert floated in mid-air in his pure form. He was a glowing sprite hovering cleanly despite the raging wind.

There was another blinding flash, twice as large as before, and the sprite turned into a bolt of lightning, moving upward. Lucas knew this phenomenon was called "ground-to-cloud-lightning." He was always exceptional at science, and that much was explainable. In the years that followed, Lucas would pioneer carbon capture biologicals, floating sheets of algae that held some of the worst effects of climate change at bay.

But what nagged at him, what wasn't explainable, and what haunted him until the day he died was why, when the clouds cleared and the day restored to its peaceful beauty, there was no sign of Gilbert. Left behind was only a tracksuit, white polyester smoldering.

The Search for Intelligent Life

by Bertram Montiekowicz

Noted UFOlogist Bolivar Sampson dedicated his life to the search for the truth, looking for any sign that alien beings had visited earth, either now or in the distant past, or perhaps in a parallel universe with multiple timelines. Sampson's financial stability and introverted lifestyle meant he could buy and read every book, attend and engage at every convention, and subscribe to any service; he even visited Roswell.

When the Internet came along Sampson dutifully uploaded his findings, and his site became a popular hub for enthusiasts. After decades in the trenches, Sampson earned the ultimate reward, a spot on Ancient Aliens' 10th Season Box Set, his "fifteen seconds of fame," as he called it, where, with a friendly smile flitting across half his face, he can be heard to say, "Poll after poll show people around the world don't trust their governments on this one same issue; if we're right, and world leaders are lying about UFOs, well, the question becomes, why would they do that?"

Sampson fell in love with his wife Ella virtually after meeting her through his website. Writing as IOU12Sampson, Ella posted curious questions to his blog. The single man, sensing the anonymous queries might be emanating from an actual woman, offered lengthy replies that revealed his determined wit. Soon their public chat became private, and they shared long missives about what it would be like if they ever had a chance to meet.

Turns out they already knew each other, but since Ella had fears and questions about her appearance, "the ultimate post traumatic stress syndrome" was how she described aging, she chose instead to build her relationship with Sampson in this way. Countless times the two lovers met without her being able to disclose the truth, in part because she liked having this one-of-a-kind insight into the great man, as both a trusted friend and suitor. She marveled at his consistency.

At MUFON 2004 they found themselves in a tight circle of mutual friends late into the night and almost the same clique reunited the same year at Contact in the Desert. In 2006, at the Science Fiction Association (SOFA) annual meeting, Sampson and Ella sat alone for a long chat about their shared ties to the UFO community. He seemed to have no clue about her true identity, even as she restated ideas they had shared in private, which seemed a little weird to her, a lack of perception on Sampson's part, and so she let the moment pass.

In 2008, as the financial crisis deepened and the president worried our sophisticated market-based economy had inexplicably lurched alongside a mysterious abyss whose powerful downward draw might prove irresistible, Ella as IOU12Sampson turned to her private chat with Sampson for solace. He reassured her, typing "ignore the rhetoric, more likely bush & co. are just emptying the coffers before riding off into the sunset" and "born again Christian blah-blah-blah, don't tell me you fell for that act," and "don't act surprised when a warmonger and torturer is also a thief." As faith in the market wavered, Sampson wrote, "when everyone's walking around like a zombie it's usually a good time to buy." "Just look at the Superbowl -- Boston and New York, that's where all these bankers live! these are their teams!!! Listen to the narrative, the New York Giants, they shouldn't even be here, how can they win? Don't write them off, like Wall Street. Somehow the undefeated and the undefeatable Tom Brady are vulnerable. OU, how much more of a hope injection do you need? Please fear not, the system will prevail." Ella decided if Sampson was right and humanity pulled away from the abyss and she happened to run into Sampson again, that would be the time to reveal her game, come what may.

For Sampson, Ella's little ruse as "OU" only endeared her to him even more, and he had tears of joy as he fell into her trap. It happened as MUFON wound down; she knew he always stayed an extra day. At breakfast, their bags packed, she steered the conversation towards one they knew well, and patiently waited for him to realize that only IOU12Sampson could be so conversant on such a topic.

Sampson liked the idea he already knew this person he had fallen in love with, "not just with emojis, alphanumeric symbols and a two-dimensional computer screen," he would say defensively, but because each partner dared to share their deepest thoughts and feelings, their dreams, what kind of parents they might be, to make promises, commitments, an organic and ever-growing crowdsourced prenuptial agreement for them to sign onto. These exchanges were among Sampson's most prized possessions and full copies of what they ever wrote to each other could be found in multiple safe spots on various media, tape, even floppy, just in case.

Although 17 years his junior, Sampson and Ella quickly married. Given she felt even more feverish about the alien presence here on earth, the married man was free to carry on with the life he built for himself, just now with a smiling bride at his side. For a moment they were the hottest couple in UFOlogy. When Ella announced her pregnancy everyone agreed their offspring could not help but become a great UFOlogist.

It's probably worth noting that Sampson himself had never seen a UFO. His interest did not stem from some inexplicable event, as opposed to many of his contemporaries, who usually claimed to have seen "something." Ella, on the other hand, remained convinced she was an alien abductee, and this is how she explained why she so rarely slept alone in the years before they were married.

One of Ella's friends at SOFA, who held multiple degrees in unrelated disciplines, presumed that since Ella felt abandoned by her parents, she invented the alien abduction story because she wanted to live in a world where she could be both helpless and ok, interesting to a higher power, and while the aliens always do with her as they please, ultimately she's returned safely, without a scratch.

Ella had a lot of strange beliefs and they all seemed to come into the frame during her brief harrowing pregnancy, which ended in disaster for everyone involved. Somehow Narnia survived and after six months left the hospital for the first time, however briefly, but by then her mother was long gone. What's crazy is that despite arguing against, disagreeing with, or ignoring every certified doctor who dared enter the room, Ella made it through, long enough to give her daughter a name, but one too many days, as it turned out. On Narnia's seventeenth day of life, Ella succumbed to a hybrid organism with no name, made immune by antibodies, indeed born of them, a monster that existed only inside the sanitized halls of Buena Suertre General Hospital. Narnia finally got home for good around the time she turned three.

Sampson doggedly carried on. He often compared himself to a machine, and the less he reflected the better he functioned. He needed the job more than ever for healthcare, as the doctors were confident Narnia would be a repeat customer. Increased responsibilities at work meant the nine-to-five stretched to six and sometimes seven, then come home to hundreds of long complex unread emails from people just like Ella, who were searching for answers, meaning in life. As far as finding anyone to replace Ella, the older he got, the less the thought crossed his mind, and that was fine; in Sampson's whole life, there would only ever be Ella.

* * *

Narnia, now 13, watched her father work, both of them bent in silence over the table. Sampson had a mini 60 Watt bulb strapped around his forehead that barely accentuated the bright light in his shop. The beam held steady on a small handmade device not yet complete. He had blue latex gloves on both hands and held a soldering gun whose power cord extended to a plug strip alongside the platform.

Sampson's closest followers in the UFO community felt his tragedy like it was their own, and perhaps selfishly worried it might render him unable to dedicate the long unpaid hours necessary to keep his site vibrant with new content; they sustained him. Money kept pouring in, and Narnia had the best schools and never an unattended moment.

As she grew, so declined Sampson's need for au pairs and chauffeurs, chaperones and concierges, valets and any of the other French words for servant. By the time Narnia turned nine Sampson managed to drive the last nurse from the house.

The two were inseparable. Whenever Sampson took the podium to address the UFO faithful, Narnia was right there in the seat behind him, taking notes. In this close-knit community, Sampson's friends bit back tears when the two approached, as Narnia looked like a miniature Ella, the same quirky Ella they had come to love, who had suffered and died because of her incredibly strong and stupid beliefs. Sampson bore his share of blame, and Ella's friends were happy to heap it on him, as he had been unable or afraid to challenge his strong-willed wife and convince her to abandon everything she believed in so she might live instead.

Sampson could not help but feel like he had to make something up to Narnia. On the worktable before him lay what he hoped would be the most special present any father could give: a device designed to communicate with aliens.

He said, "You see how this completes the connection." Sampson flashed the beam from the device to a line art diagram on an open page; almost all of the pages had been turned around the black plastic coils of the textbook's GBC Binding. "Obviously, it's not going to do anything until we add power."

Narnia, her brow furrowed as always, nodded, and she fit her protective glasses in place as Sampson soldered the last two wires together.

With gloved hand, he turned one page and then another. "The rest is just footnotes and glossary and what-not." He stood straight and pulled the strap from his graying head to click off the light. "It's done."

She said, "Ok, I'll finish packing."

Within a half hour they were on the road, Sampson's 2012 Subaru Outback loaded. The device from the worktable had been wrapped in a variety of materials to both guarantee its safety and protect it from any known scanning devices that might be along the road or at the toll stations, or perhaps used by helicopters flying silently above, military aircraft, satellites, or UFOs themselves. The instructions in their GBC Binding had been resealed and mailed to himself with no return address; Sampson didn't want the textbook in the car or unattended at the house. As the miles unfurled he searched through every radio station while Narnia watched the world blur by.

As planned, he guided the Subaru off the highway at the second overlook, the Great Pass, and as usual this late in the day they found an empty picnic table. Sampson and Narnia each packed their own meal, but they were remarkably similar.

As a UFOlogist it was common for Sampson to come into contact with conspiracy theorists who agreed with even the most unprovable aspects of his theories, seeing everything he believed as part of a bigger narrative, that the presence of alien life was just one facet of hidden truth. It could be said Ella fit this description, but there were many more further beyond her on the continuum, and as the Internet continued to grow, it seemed more were always coming.

What Sampson learned is that while these conspiracy theorists might embrace a wide range of ideas, one truth they all seemed to agree upon is that eating processed food was no good for you. Sampson ate what he could trust, what he grew for himself, and their bunker was well stocked. He dropped $2,500 on a water purification system and his financial backers didn't bat an eye. They wanted him to be safe and happy.

He watched Narnia pick about the various foodstuffs she had gathered. "Did you throw that pumpkin in the compost?"

She looked up in mock horror. "I totally forgot."

He pictured the critters crawling around the yard, the mess, fighting for bounty, but swallowed the petty resentment. He spoiled her, but can you blame him? She had survived, and as long as Narnia was there, he didn't need to remember Ella, because he could never forget her.

Sampson and Narnia packed up and were back on the road after one long last look at the fiery majesty of the setting sun, burning smoky, the sky, pixelated bars of pink bleeding to purple behind dusty sequin colored clouds. They still had almost another hour before their exit and at least one more after that on 133 before the final leg up Ridge Road. Sampson's house was only five hours from one of the most high traffic areas for UFO sightings in all of California.

As they turned onto Ridge Road he engaged the high beams, as there were no lights out here this close to the ocean. He grew serious.

"Maybe we should go over the questions again."

Without a word Narnia opened her large hand-sewn purse, drawing forth a piece of three-hole loose leaf paper folded in four. She took a moment as she prepared to read, pausing after each question.

"Question One: 'Are you God?'. Question Two: 'What are your plans for the human race?'"

They proceeded through the list with practiced ease and it passed the time nicely. When they arrived at the campsite, Sampson popped the hatchback and slid the telescope out of the way so he could grab the tent bag. A couple other smaller bags and the cooler followed, resting on the ground.

"Dad?"

"Yeah?"

"Maybe we should use the communicator first and then set up camp."

He looked at her for a long moment. "Ok." He dug out the device they had created in the workshop, concealed beneath the camping gear. With trembling hands he peeled away the lead blanket and other camouflage until the first wires appeared.

She asked, "Can I hold it?"

"Just keep it in the box."

She took the innocent-looking cardboard and stepped back as Sampson refilled the Subaru, leaving the telescope draped across the front seat. Finally, he slung the portable table over his shoulder. He looked around cautiously before locking the car. There were two other vehicles in the small lot, both older models.

He said, "Ok, let's go. I should carry it, I think. I want to keep it as level as possible."

"Let me take the table then."

They exchanged burdens and marched off along the familiar trail. The path led up the ridge to where the campground overlooked the sea. They continued past the curious campers who offered a friendly wave. The trail wound up and around to a second campground that sat on the Angelina Plateau overlooking Grand Valley. It was on this second section of trail that countless visitors had reported strange lights that shot off over the Pacific or hovered near the DARPA installation on St. Simeon Island. In 1984 two Pan Am stewardesses on Flight 167 reported being tracked for nearly three minutes by a formation of triangle shaped lights that came out of the San Juniata Desert to hover just below where Sampson and Narnia now stood, the spot they chose to use the communicator.

Narnia deftly arranged the table and Sampson tested the weight with his elbow before setting the device in place. He didn't know what to say, so he said, "Well, this is it." He plugged in the nine-volt battery.

Early in his career Sampson had the opportunity to intern with Doctor of Music Appreciation Arthur Anderson, who became a leading advocate for the theory alien communication would have nothing to do with voices and that whatever we said probably sounded like a dog bark or a bird whistle; more likely the aliens would speak in mathematics, but Dr. Anderson advocated music as another possibility, given its mathematical qualities.

When Dr. Anderson presented his theory at SOFA, one of the attendees pointed him to a short story called Starlight Rhapsody by Valentina Zhuravleva, originally written in Russian, which was translated into English for the January 1964 issue of Fantasy and Science Fiction Magazine. Zhuravleva was married to Genrich Altshuler, the intellectual behind the Theory of Inventive Problem Solving (TRIZ) and Founder of the Azerbaijan Public Institute for Inventive Creation. It had been Altshuler who, as a young man, after searching for ways to measure inventiveness, compiled his findings in a personal letter that he mailed to Josef Stalin. The dictator was so impressed with the 22-year-old's work he threw him into a labor camp. When Altshuler emerged, supposedly cured of his intellectual pursuits, he began writing science fiction instead. Some UFOlogists saw this as evidence Altshuler had chosen this medium to reveal what he learned about aliens while imprisoned alongside the other great thinkers of his time, who as prisoners were free to share their opinion, and as Russians were immune to any US-led cover-up, psy-op or limited hang-out.

In Starlight Rhapsody, the aliens use musical notes to communicate with humanity, simply by varying the isotopes on a spectrogram and patterning them off Mendeleev's periodic table, which is broken into eight parts, like octaves. Anderson, however, believed true communication would require not just two dimensional notes from a piece of paper, but a third dimension, resonance, a statistic he struggled to quantify. Anderson believed the ancients built massive stone structures because they knew how to distort gravity using sound waves, but despite spending millions of dollars he could not repeat the feat with a replica he built of the drum and horn kit discovered at the King's Temple in Lankmar.

Dr. Anderson appeared on one of the earliest UFO documentaries, "When Gods Ruled Earth." No one could say where the funding had come from, but after appearing on a local cable channel no longer in existence, Prism, When Gods Ruled Earth found eternal life on the Internet, despite numerous attempts to have it taken down for some of its more heretical claims. Conspiracy theorists long posited that this censorship is the best evidence When Gods Ruled Earth must have gotten something right. In his section, Anderson, filmed on site in Lankmar, asks, "How could anyone, man or God, alien or monster, stack 60-ton granite slabs like those found above the King's Chamber in the Great Pyramid, without the least appreciation of acoustics?"

Anderson at first seemed in a state of shock when word spread the young director Steven Spielberg had decided to leverage his success with Jaws to make a UFO movie, that Hynek was involved, and that they had effectively stolen his idea as the driver of the plot. When Anderson heard Spielbert hired John Williams, who displaced Anderson as Los Angeles' resident musical prodigy prodigy when he transferred to North Hollywood High School from New York in 1948, how could he not sense the Powers That Be were working in concert to derail his work, to make a mockery of everything he had fought so hard to prove. When Anderson first heard five note sing song melody Williams had composed, he flew in a rage, prophetically predicting that he would be completely forgotten while Spielberg would become a household name. Fantasy and Science Fiction Magazine published Anderson's complaints in its Letter to the Editor section, under the title, "How could it be so simple?" where he wrote in part, "the aliens would have received so many messages from earth by now they must feel like changing the channel."

Dr. Anderson's appointment as Dean of Music History at the University of California at Santa Anna Diego garnered the patina of professional scholarship UFOlogists so desperately needed. This resulted in U-SAD becoming the repository for some of the best audio evidence ever recorded. The archive includes the 1982 Dunfee Tape, where 19-year-old Charley Dunfee used a battery operated hand-held Panasonic recorder to capture on cassette the first instance of what is now known as the Anderson Signal. The AS on the Dunfee Tape can also be heard on the so-called Harrot File, a digital recording collected in 2020 by Mary and Madison Harrot from the very spot where Sampson and his daughter Narnia now stood. Of course Anderson had died in 2011, so the Harrot File went instead to Professors Pintor and Macaul, who were serving as co-chairs of the Anderson Institute. In both the Dunfee Tape and the Harrot File the AS can be heard with the same clarity, but it was not until the digital recording that Lindor and Macaul were able to identify the sound's exact resonance coordinates and plot the sounds in 3D using the vague terms provided by Anderson. Just last month, Pintor disappeared after Macaul committed suicide; before going underground, Pintor sent the findings to Sampson, describing how anyone might build a device capable of replicating the AS. Sampson made arrangements for the instructions to be published, but decided to build the device himself first. As far as he knew, tonight would be the first test of what Lindor and Macaul labeled the N1 Alien Communicator (NAC).

It's dangerous to ascribe too much or too little to the thirteen-year-old brain. In children's stories the fairy godmother takes you on a magical journey; this is how Narnia understood her mother's obsession with UFO abduction, which Ella's friends could not help but describe in great detail. Narnia, having spent so much of her life among UFOlogists, calling them Uncle and Aunt, had come to believe the pursuit of UFOs as no different than the search for God, like Sir Isaac Newton with his head buried in the Bible, looking for patterns, and finding them. No one wants to accept a mundane life, especially the brilliant; if you're smart you want to learn something new.

The modern world into which she had been born held plenty of contradiction. Some people believed in science and God. Others believed in God without ever going to church. In America freedom of religion had been around so long no one seemed to know what it meant anymore, assuming it meant you were free to believe whatever you want.

Narnia looked up expectantly after her father used the communicator to create a striking rendition of the Anderson Signal. To her surprise one of the countless stars in the sky took flight, growing in luminosity. The circle of her eye grew, round like the craft. Narnia didn't even notice her father had lost consciousness until he slumped to the side and crumbled on the path, rolling somewhat towards the cliff. She could see he was still breathing, with a blissful smile on his face.

"Dad!" By then both he and the craft had stopped, closeby.

The hatch opened, quick steps on the landing ramp. With her unconscious father on the ground at her feet, Narnia looked up to behold the alien, backlit by the dull light falling from inside the flying saucer. The being that emerged, a middle-aged woman, seemed irate.

"He's fine. What are you doing, kid?"

Narnia tried to comprehend the mixed signals, assuming the alien could take a form her eyes would find comforting, that its language abilities allowed her to understand as if it spoke in her native tongue.

Mouth dry, Narnia followed her training. "Are you God?"

"Hah!" The woman seemed like she wanted to laugh. "You're serious? D'you know what you've just done? You sent a distress signal, like dialing 911. Don't ever do it again, ok?"

Robotically, Narnia asked, "What are your plans for the people of earth?"

"What are you talking about, kid? We are the people of earth. There's no plans."

Narnia was well-versed in numerous theories that imagine UFOs might be terrestrial in nature, either because they were part of some quasi-government elite, were here for thousands or perhaps millions of years before humans, or had originated somewhere else but now call earth home. Since the middle-aged woman did not wear a uniform or flaunt a weapon, and the craft seemed only large enough for one, Narnia concluded the occupant felt like earth was already under her control.

Determined, Narnia stuck with the script. "Where did you come from?"

The woman cracked a smile. "Over there." She pointed sarcastically to the point in the sky where Narnia had first seen the light approach. "I'm human, just like you. There's no difference between me and you, except you're the kind of person who crank calls 911." The older woman did an about-face on the exit ramp.

Panicked, Narnia could not remember the next question and then any of the questions. Caught in the moment as it seemed like she would be left behind, she blurted, "Do you believe in God?"

This stopped the woman in her tracks and she turned to face the child. "You're pretty interested in God I see. Here's what I want you to do. Take every religious text, put all the words and concepts into a computer, and ask the AI to write a New Bible, and in this Bible, it only includes the consensus found in every religion. Now, what do you have? You'd have essentially a condensed version of the same book everybody already worships. There's nothing to fight about, people brought that to religion. The messages from God are the same. Don't lie, don't cheat, don't kill, don't fantasize about your neighbor's wife." The woman stopped herself, gesturing towards the flying saucer. "If you don't mind."

Narnia, her mind blank, could only think of one other question, one she herself had lobbied to have added and which Sampson grudgingly left at the end of the list. "What do you do for fun?"

The woman paused again, this time in the entryway. "Really? You want to know what I do for fun?" She let out a little laugh. "What I do for fun, is, I live." She jerked as if to go.

"But wait! We have so many questions. Please don't leave! You wouldn't want me to misunderstand you, would you? You wouldn't want me to tell the story in such a way as to paint you in a light you don't want to be painted in!"

The woman gave Narnia a long look, and for the first time looked down at her father, who smilingly rested his head on a rock. "Oh my God, Bolivar Sampson. I should have known. Would you please tell him to just leave us alone. Why does he even care what we do or think?"

"Let us tell your story!"

A sarcastic snarl curled into place. "You want everyone to know about UFOs, hunh? That's funny, that's really funny. Ok, I'll tell you. You people are suffering down here on earth, in what we call hell. You spend a trillion dollars on a meaningless war, we don't even have dollars; what do you really need dollars for? I mean, shouldn't everybody have what they need? While at the same time other people have more than they need? Think about it. Is that really a society. Sounds more like a scam."

Narnia stared for a long moment. "You're serious, you're just regular people?"

"What did you think I was going to have a big head, big old brain sticking out. Nah, just a person. Sorry to disappoint you."

"But—."

"Choices, kid, choices; what's life but choices? I'm sure you have a couple dollars in your pocket right now, what are you going to do with it? You going to buy some candy that rots your teeth? You going to give it to some homeless vet so you can feel better about sending him off to fight for oil, then he takes your dollars and buys poison so he can shoot it into his veins and then that way he can feel better about being sent off to a war nobody else even cares about. No one remembers what he can't forget. Once you have these dollars, then the next question is, what are you going to do with them. That same dollar can spread pain or joy, or both. It's a choice. This is nothing new. Only the scale is different, billions, trillions. What are you guys, 30 trillion in debt? Oh man what a mess. So you see, the dollars you use are like Monopoly money. It's all a big joke."

"But, how, I mean, if you are from a breakaway society, how did you do it?"

"We have to go back hundreds of years here. What do we got all night? You seem like a smart kid. You know back in the 1700s and 1800s, when humanity started coming up with these inventions, what people were saying. It was all like, 'Wow, think how this is gonna elevate the human race. With technology, no one will ever need to work again!'" Her voice continued to rise. "'Everyone will live longer, healthier lives, there will be no war, no poor, no hungry, no malady, humanity will be free to pursue its happiness, make love and art! Technology will solve all our problems!' Ha, ha, ha. So what happened? What went wrong? How can productivity be up and wages stagnant? Ask yourself that. If technology made you twice as productive you should be paid twice as much, right? Simple mathematics. Well either that or you should work half as much, or retire sooner, none of which is happening, the opposite is happening. So don't be amazed our society used technology to better the lives of everyone, be amazed yours didn't. How hard you had to work to make sure not everyone benefits. That was what we did, not you, us, our ancestors, not yours. That's how we conquered space and the skies. But there were some who didn't agree, see? Your JP Morgan types. They said, wait, we can't give technology away, someone has to profit. And if someone must profit, someone must starve. If we want a world with winners, each must be surrounded by a hundred losers, and that number just keeps going up. The technology will be deployed on the masses, but not for their benefit. So what does that mean to you? Lies, lies, lies, lies, lies, lies, lies. But we humans have to believe in something, right? It's part of our DNA, so we have no choice, we start believing in lies. Rinse and repeat for a hundred years or so, and now everybody believes the same lies, your father, your grandfather. You've never met anyone who knows the truth. No one trusts anyone to tell the truth, and for good reason! And then men like your father come along, and they say, 'Wait, something's missing!' Of course something's missing! The humanity! 'One day the world will be so rotted we can start selling water and air.'" The woman regained her composure to glare at Narnia in disdain. "Look at you... pathetic. Following these fake little clues about UFOs while the real conspiracies are right out in the open. I can't imagine living in your world, settling for it. And you can't imagine living in mine, achieving it. What would your father do if he were freed from the pressures of his meaningless job, if there were no papers to push, no bills to pay, no rivalries to contest, no one to feign superiority over, if there was no damage to the environment, and everything hung in perfect balance; what would you do? You would travel and enjoy this beautiful magical planet and everything it has to offer, the company of strangers, the most healthy diet and lifestyle." The woman caught herself again. "Like any good tourist, we do our best to avoid the natives, they're such brutes; so, if you don't mind?" She took a final step inside the doorway, now outlined in the craft's gray glow, just like in the movie.

Narnia reached out to her. "But, don't you have a message for me, something I can share with my father. He, I think all these years, he wanted to believe mostly out of hope, that there's someone out there powerful enough to save us from ourselves. Maybe he wasn't wrong!"

"Tell your father he's an idiot." The sinister chuckle returned. "Hope? That's what you want from me? You hope I'm going to save you? You should be worried about saving me. Don't you think we would have remade the world in our image if we could? Might makes right, eh? There's no nobility in nobility. You want me to shoot somebody with a laser? You don't get it, do you? You put me at great risk by using that thing, all of our kind. I would love to see you destroy it right now, but I'm not going to make you. I'm not going to use my superior technology to overwhelm you. That's the difference between my society and yours: I'm not prepared to kill you because we don't agree. Why do you think the most brilliant nations do nothing but develop new weapons, why the richest men are rocketing into space? They're looking for us, and you're helping them. One day, they're going to figure out a way to kill us, as surely as they killed the idea that technology means everyone prospers together. No, happiness is class-based. As you can so plainly see, in your world, it is those who care the least who get to wield power the most. No wonder you have so many problems. Politicians are short-sighted liars so yeah, let's put them in charge."

Narnia tried to control her confusion. It had been her idea to write out the questions, to save humanity, but now she realized its fate was controlled by choices, and who gets to make them. Head held high, eyes red-rimmed, she asked, "But don't you think you could help us? You would prove it was possible to live a happier life."

"Come on, kid, we gave up on earthlings a long time ago. No one changes their mind, precisely because you're trying to change their mind. They assume you must have some interest, otherwise why bother? I could fly up on live TV right now and everyone would think it's a guerrilla marketing campaign for some stupid movie."

Narnia held back the tears. "But, I bet you could get people to change their minds if you tried."

"Listen to yourself. You're like, what, 10? Let me give you some advice. To succeed in your world, don't keep it real. Don't be yourself. Don't let everyone get to know you a little better. That's not going to help. Instead, craft an image of a successful happy you, and portray that image to every set of eyes and especially every camera that's ever pointed your way. Ninety-nine times out of a hundred the lie is more palatable. At this point, you expect to be lied to, it's like a societal convention. Let me ask you this since we're having our little chat. Do you believe the official government story about what happened on 9/11? Do you think Donald Trump was elected president? Isn't it weird that, for those unreal events, Rudy Guiliani cast himself in the role of public servant? Believe what you want to believe, everyone will. Just turn on the news. If you don't like the world you live in, change the channel, and find a new world waiting. Somebody must be lying. Surprise! It's both, but what do you expect from a news show? Its popularity is based on the quantity and quality of lies on offer. News show hosts don't want to inform, just enrage, that's how they make money. I mean these shows are so stupid. The hosts, night after night, with their phony outrage. The same guests appearing over and over just to tell the host, "you're right, you're right." All because it's a cheap and effective method of spreading hate. They love their country, but hate everybody in it. Face it, kid, as long as one person has hate in their heart for anyone else, what chance do earthlings have of building a happy future? Hatred of our fellow man is what every God warned us against from the dawn of time. If you're looking for God and the meaning of life, go back and look at the ancient texts. You guys are looking for God in the wrong place. Just open your eyes for Christ's sake. Creation. It's a beautiful thing."

Sampson grunted.

"Well, that's my cue. Good luck, kid. Don't ever let them tell you one person can't change the world. That's the biggest lie they want you to believe." The woman stepped inside the circular craft and after the landing ramp silently sealed, purred off into the night sky.

In the campground below someone shouted, "Oh my God, did you see that?"

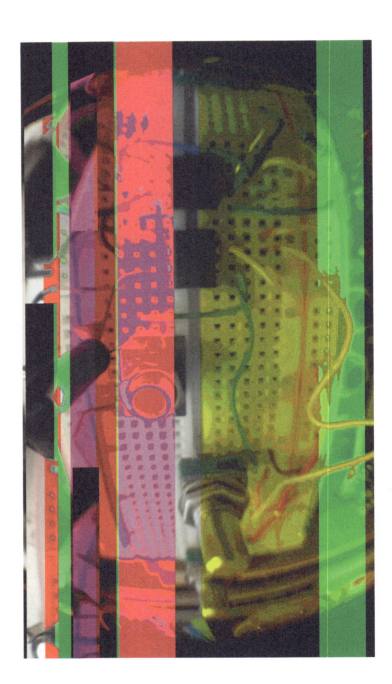

The Stripper Story

by Jackrabbit

Kane shouted half to his friends and half to the club, a smile cutting its way across his bearded face. "Goddamn, it's good to be home again."

He'd just paid the cover for himself and his friend Jake—his arm close over Jake's shoulders in an almost headlock.

The rest of Kane's friends were lined up at the door getting their IDs checked and forking over the entrance fee.

Kane hooted as he and Jake passed through the inner door and were immersed in Led Zeppelin's Tangerine and the pink and blue lights cascading down from the ceiling. Jake grinned along with Kane, but kept quiet, allowing the arm Kane had draped over his shoulder to corral him alongside.

To their left a long stage split the club at a diagonal starting at a far corner and ending in the middle of the floor. Two women danced naked as other semi-nude women solicited groups of men lining the stage.

As they waited for the rest of the crew to catch up, Kane turned to Jake, "Bro, let me buy you a lap dance. You totally deserve it for turning us on to this place."

Jake gave Kane a smile that tasted bitter.

"That's, ok, Kane. I appreciate it, but I'm good. Thanks, though." He looked over Kane's shoulder and gestured, "Isn't that Viper over there at the bar?"

Like a golden retriever catching a glimpse of a chipmunk racing through the underbrush, Kane's eyes widened as he looked around, "Oh yeah?" He grinned.

Having successfully targeted the young woman, Kane turned back to his friend. "Ok, Jake, you just take a couple bucks and if you change your mind, remember: we are here to have some fun, yes?" Kane handed Jake a bottle of Budwiser from the twelve-pack he held under his arm. "I have no idea how you found a BYOB stripclub, but you deserve a Nobel Prize for it."

Then he dug in his pockets, pulling out bills for his friends. "Have a good time and find me if you need anything."

Jake watched Kane walk away and get almost tackled on his way to the bar by the rest of his friends.

He envied them their good time.

But strip clubs were supposed to be fun, right? Was he unhappy because of the looming specter of capitalism or undiagnosed depression?

Pondering this question, he found an empty table away from the stage and plopped himself into a chair. Kane wanted him to have a good time, he told himself, so he may as well enjoy the view.

Almost immediately after he sat down a woman he didn't recognize sat down next to him—close enough that her naked thigh rubbed against his pants. "Hi, Papi! How you doin' tonight? My name's Gabrielle," she smiled. Jake thought her caramel skin and accent sounded Brazilian. He came often enough to recognize a handful of the dancers, some by name, but Gabrielle was a new face at FantasyLand. He expected new faces when he visited. Employee retention was not a characteristic of the adult entertainment industry he was familiar with.

"I'm Jake," he said.

Gabrielle shared a knowing smile with him. "So, you here to have some fun tonight, Jake?"

She was one of the more conventionally beautiful women working at the club. Tall and lithe, she glowed and sparkled as she leaned into him with youthful eagerness.

Too eager, Jake noted.

It was part of the game to be enthusiastic about sitting next to a club patron. As part of the game he didn't take it personally.

"Do you like being called Gabby, Gabrielle?" Jake asked. He thought he could see a hint of a smile.

"People call me Gab."

"How are you tonight, Gab?" His smile was disarming and genuine.

"I'm ok, Jake. It's been a long week." Gabrielle's shoulders relaxed by a little.

"Oh yeah? What's going on? What made it so long?" Now he leaned in to show her he was eager to hear what she had to say.

"Oh my God, Papi, my girlfriend has been driving me crazy! She thinks she isn't good enough to be with me." Gab looked frustrated. "I keep telling her we're great together, but she just keeps pulling away from me."

"Oh, I'm sorry to hear that. I relate." Jake didn't mention that he related to Gabrielle's girlfriend. "Does she apologize all the time?" He asked.

"Even for things she has nothing to do with!" She gave him an exasperated look, "She apologized to my shoes this morning when she kicked one of them walking to the bathroom."

"Oof. That's a bit much," he said with a smile.

Gab took a breath. She smiled and recalibrated, focusing on Jake. "You're cute, Jake. But, you look like you've got something on your mind. Are you having a good time?"

"Of course I am!" Jake did his best to raise his energy level to hers, "I love this place. I brought my friends here because it's so great." He gestured to the group of young well groomed men seated by the stage. "That's my friend Kane," he pointed to his friend, who had separated himself from the larger group. Like Jake, Kane was sitting at a table away from the stage. Kane was also talking to a woman, the woman Jake had pointed out when they'd entered the club, Viper. "We're out tonight for his bachelor party."

Gabrielle perked up, "Ooh, Papi! Let's get him up on stage!" She smiled and shook a little in her seat as she grabbed Jake's forearm and gave it a squeeze.

"I'll give you guys a nice show. He'll be thinking about me the whole time he's at the altar!"

"That would be so cool, Gab, but this is our second time here this weekend." Jake sounded conciliatory, "Last night we got Kane up on stage with Viper and she took us all to the School Room along with Cassidy. Kane was a very bad student, and I can confirm he had a very good time. I'm sorry," he said again.

"Well what about you, Papi?" Gabrielle leaned in closer to Jake so that he could smell fresh strawberries. "Do you want to have a 'very good time'?" She put her hand on his leg and gave it a light squeeze. "I like boys, too, Jake. How about I give you a lap dance for free?"

When negotiating with dancers, this was the point at which Jake would be reminded of his ex. She'd been a stripper. It embarrassed him to think of the person he was when they dated. He'd only gone to see her at work once, and had been heartbroken to see her dehumanized while she was up on that stage. He felt himself turning her into a gyrating meat doll along with the rest of the club's patrons. Something for strangers to lust after, with no thought to the person beneath the surface. That was when the mask of eroticism had been pulled away from desaturated reality. He would always see the dancer as a complete human being, and the dynamic at a club—like the one he was at now—as capitalism's collateral damage.

Gab wasn't his plaything. She was full of history and complexities he couldn't begin to imagine. It felt like disrespect to do anything outside of honoring that humanity.

"No thank you, Gab, but here, thanks for talking to me." Jake pulled a twenty away from the cash Kane had given him and handed it to the dancer. She took it from his hand and stood up.

"Ok, you have a good night, Papi." She leaned down to give him a kiss on the cheek, "You're a good listener," she said and smiled, before turning to walk away.

He knew it was all just a perversion of human relationships processed through the meatgrinder of commodification, but he sympathized with his friends.

He could see the appeal of simple conversations started with no effort. The absence of anxiety that came from not having to risk your self esteem over a perfect stranger at a house party or a bar. No pressure to be handsome or rich or clever. No need to be anything more than what you were. What more could a guy want but to feel like it was fine just to be himself and have that be enough?

Jake checked on the guys he came with. He didn't know any of them before he met them this weekend. They were Kane's friends. Good guys. He liked them all, but he had to admit to himself tonight was a pretty standard bachelor party vibe. Three or four groups of red-blooded American men in addition to his own were positioned around the stage, tossing small bills at the dancers. Disco balls turned. Multi-colored club lights washed over the space. Music chosen by the woman dancing blared from the speakers.

As part of the weekend-long bachelor party, the group of them had stopped at a different stripclub earlier that evening—The Tits Ahoy Lounge. Kane's brother bought him a public lap dance from a woman who looked like a very skinny, very tattooed, very pierced Vampira.

Jake recalled the scene with discomfort. He'd wondered why the bouncer was standing there after handcuffing Kane's hands behind his back. Jake thought it might have been for the protection of the performer? But, after watching Vampira tear open Kane's shirt and pull out his chest hairs Jake was pretty sure the bouncer was there to protect the customer from her. The rest of the "dance" was Vampira violently slamming her body against Kane in one of the least appealing displays of public humiliation Jake had seen since the Folsom Street Fair in San Francisco.

Kane demanded they all take a taxi back to FantasyLand as soon as he was released from the stage. He seemed to have recovered from his Tits Ahoy experience. The man of the hour was still at the table to Jake's right, flirting with Viper.

Jake thought back to last night and the "lesson" Viper had given Kane.

They had arrived at FantasyLand and immediately Jake had walked up to the bartender to consult her about the evening's activities. "Hi Nix, how have you been?"

"I'm good. Hey, have you seen this crazy video?" Nix pulled her phone out from her bra where she had it stored, and after pulling up a video, proffered it to Jake. He watched a young man at a crowded pool attempting to dive off a cooler and failing miserably as a pool full of his friends laughed. "Can you believe that idiot?" She asked him.

"Nuts," he said. "Hey, I'm here with a bachelor party tonight and I was wondering what you recommend."

"Oh, you should ask for Ginger and Molotov to do a show for you in the School Room," she replied.

By the time the bachelor party had come to an agreement Kane had chosen Viper and her co-worker Chastity.

Along with one of the club's bouncers the two girls led the entire crew to a room adjacent to the main club. There were a few of these rooms, most of them unmarked. The door they were entering, however, had a neon sign over it announcing "School" in cursive with an arrow pointing down.

Inside was a desk at one end of the room, a few school chairs facing it, and at the other end of the room a well-worn couch.

The women sat Kane down in one of the chairs. Viper sat next to him, taking on the role of his fellow student, and Chastity stood at the desk, playing the part of concerned teacher.

What followed was a scene involving Kane's punishment for getting caught under the bleachers with Viper. After getting spanked by both women, Chastity in the teacher role instructed Kane on how to properly pleasure his new friend, Viper. Jake and the rest hooted, laughed, and yowled at Kane until they were asked to leave the room. Everyone except for Kane was politely escorted out by the stone-faced bouncer.

Kane didn't share with his friends what had transpired after the door closed with him still inside.

That had been last night. Now it was Saturday. Jake felt self-conscious and a little envious as he watched Kane lean into Viper. She whispered something into his ear and the two of them got up from the table. Viper took Kane's hand and led him through a door on the far side of the stage from where Jake was sitting.

As the door closed behind them, Jake slumped back in his chair and surveyed the floor. He noted a feeling of isolation which he found curious considering he was surrounded by people and activity. There was a sense that time was a series of peaks and valleys and his timeline was either a second early or a second late relative to everyone else in the club. He was alone in a club whose sole purpose was making social connections. He felt defeated.

Movement in his peripheral vision caused him to turn his head. His eyes caught on a woman standing by herself off to the side of the long stage. She was tall with long red hair and wore a revealing dancer's outfit. She stood with arms-crossed watching an athletic, black, heavily tattooed woman whip her large afro around to the beat of Public Enemy's Fight the Power. The DJ's voice boomed through the PA, "Let's give it up for MOLOTOV!" The nude Molotov held a fist in the air, violently gyrating to the music under a hail of crumpled dollar bills thrown at her by the men lining the stage.

Jake looked back to the woman and was surprised to find her staring at him.

In that moment Jake was keenly aware of his self imposed isolation but also a relaxing of that feeling of aloneness. It was a welcome relief, however slight, and he felt compelled to get up from his seat to interrogate this change in mood with the red-haired woman.

He shuffled over to her so that they were both facing the stage.

"Hi, my name's Jake," he said while turning his head to look at her.

The woman turned about 45 degrees to look down at Jake. "Hi, Jake. It's nice to meet you. I'm Ginger," she held her hand out to him, "an alien."

Jake's eyes brightened slightly as he took the offered hand and squeezed it gently, "I've heard about you," he said with a grin and introduced himself.

Ginger's left eyebrow raised slightly along with the corner of her mouth, "Oh really?"

"Yes! I asked the bartender who we should have perform for my friend's private dance and you were one of the girls she suggested. But, Kane kind of has a thing for Viper so we decided to go with her."

Ginger sniffed and the playful look subsided from her face. "Hm. I'm not surprised. Viper's young and thin. You guys missed out, though." The wry smile returned to her face. "Maybe you can reconsider your choice for his second marriage." She went back to watching the girls dancing on the stage with naked abandon.

"I'm sorry Ginger, did you just say you're an alien?"

She didn't change her orientation, but remained watching the stage with her arms crossed, "I was hooked on speed when I was living in San Francisco and getting my masters in urban planning." She paused to sigh. Jake was about to ask a question but stopped himself. "I've been clean for years now," she went on, "but it's given me a certain perspective dancing here. For example, I hosted a clinic for the girls on how to use naloxone."

Jake took note of the way that some recovering addicts tended to overshare and that a woman could be a stripper and pursue higher education. But, he felt awkward. Sharing intimate details of her personal life with a stranger seemed commonplace to Ginger. Was he the one with the problem? In an age of social media was he the odd man out because he thought personal things shouldn't be public knowledge?

Those questions aside, he was impressed with Ginger's frankness. Impressed and concerned. "Wait, Naloxone is the drug you use for people who OD on opioids, isn't it? Have girls OD'd here?"

"I haven't seen any myself since I've been here, but there's been drama in the past." She paused to put a finger to the side of her mouth, "I am worried about Paisley, though. She seems like she's having a hard time with her demons."

Jake was feeling out of phase again. But a subtle sense of being on the same timeline as Ginger was scaring him. He knew she was a whole person, but he used the protocol of dancer versus customer as a defense against having to expose his own humanity. He would use the money he handed off at the end of a conversation as a stand in for his own authentic feelings.

He reached for something to say that might cover up the discomfort growing in the shadows of his thoughts. "What role do you think capitalism plays into the commodification of people's relationships here? Doesn't it turn a touch or a smile into a product?"

"I think the money in your pocket is a way to keep from feeling something, Jake. What is it you want to ask me?"

Her question felt like a challenge he was willing to meet. Despite being intimidating, she was genuine. "I'm wondering why I feel so alone in a place like this, surrounded by all these people."

Ginger responded without hesitation, as if she knew he was going to say this.

"You've heard that men are from mars and women are from venus, right?"

Jake nodded.

"Well, it's true. Mostly. Men and women are aliens living together on earth's surface. Guys don't know how to talk to women and women don't know how to talk to men. That's where I come in. I'm the alien translator. I mean, seriously. Take a look." Ginger gestured to the room. "This place may as well be the cantina from Star Wars."

The colored lights shining down from the ceiling made everything near the stage look pink or purple. Lynyrd Skynyrd blared from the speakers. Jake noticed that Kat had taken the stage.

During another of his visits to FantasyLand, Kat had confessed to Jake she was a recovering addict who hoped to work out a way to see her child more than once every other weekend. It was going to be hard since she was a felon now, having been convicted of transporting drugs for her dealer.

Jake was reminded of the show Squid Game while he and Kat had talked over a drink.

Because of her felony conviction, Kat was having a hard time finding work outside the club. There were only so many opportunities open to her. She was struggling to get her life together and tonight getting her life together looked like lying supine with her legs in the air slowly torquing back and forth, the meat of her thighs waving along the bone and connective tissue. Men sitting at the edge of the stage aimed crumpled dollar bills at her exposed sex, shouting their gutteral appreciation.

He couldn't have imagined a world more alien to the one outside the club's doors.

He looked back at Ginger to let her know he understood what she was implying. "This isn't like any other place most Americans experience in the course of their day," he said.

"No," she said. "But not because girls like me walk around naked. It's not like any other place because it's a place where men come to speak to aliens." She closed the gap between them with a slight bend at her waist. "Jake, these men here don't know how to talk to the women in their lives." She pointed to a man in a pink polo shirt and a fifty dollar haircut who had his hand around Gabrielle's waist. "That guy over there can't talk to his wife about how badly he wants to change jobs." She gestured to another man who was dressed in a leather jacket and was laughing along with his fellows. "That guy is ashamed of his kinks and won't let his girlfriend know he likes to wear high-heels and fishnets." Now she was indicating one of the men in Kane's party he'd come to the club with, "That one over there doesn't know how to break up with his partner because he doesn't want to hurt her feelings. I bet they're together for another year or two and very unhappy." She looked back to Jake. "These men talk to me because I'm a woman they won't scare off with their vulnerabilities. They know they're not going to offend me or tell me something I haven't heard a million times before. I'm not available to them outside of the club, so there's no pressure to impress me."

"You're like their counselor," Jake looked up into Ginger's eyes, bewildered.

"Jake, we learned our times tables in elementary school and science, and the most dumbed down version of American history imaginable. But, when did we learn about what it takes to have a good conversation? How not to be an asshole? How to be a good listener?" She waited for him to answer.

"We didn't."

"No," she echoed, "we didn't. Every single one of those kids in your class were going to have relationships. Every. One. They would have all benefited from learning the basics of what goes into a successful relationship. Instead we were schooled into whatever flavor of dysfunction our family had for us. Outside of our family's mess we got popular culture. What's your favorite movie, Jake?"

The answer was at the top of Jake's mind and he answered almost as soon as Ginger finished asking her question, "Blade Runner. It's been my favorite movie since I was 13. My dad took me to see it."

Ginger laughed out loud as she threw her thin white arm around Jake's shoulders. "Jake, you gave me the perfect example, thank you." She angled her head closer to his as she spoke, "There is a scene in that movie that is presented as very romantic. Sexy music swells as the two leads stare into each other's eyes as they start a passionate kiss." Ginger was slowly moving towards Jake as she described the scene. Now she pulled back. "Do you know the scene I'm referring to?"

Jake at 13 had been very excited watching Deckard and Rachel get it on. He nodded that he understood what she was talking about.

"Go back and watch that scene again. Notice that Harrison Ford won't let Sean Young leave his apartment. She's upset and she's trying to get out but he slams the door on her and blocks her escape." Ginger continued as she grabbed both of Jake's shoulders, "He's much bigger than she is. He grabs her and violently throws her against the wall. She looks terrified. With an intense look in his eye, and no sign of willingness from her, he closes in on her and kisses her. Then he orders her to ask for him to continue, which she does." She paused and let her hands fall to her sides.

"Did your dad tell you that scene was sexual abuse, Jake?"

Jake looked at the floor, ashamed. "No. I thought it was romantic."

"Sure you did, baby. Ridley Scott is a great director and he manipulated you into thinking abuse is sexy. And your dad went along with it." She smiled and threw a playful punch at his shoulder. "You didn't know the difference between abuse and romance, but you sure did know your multiplication tables, didn't you, Jake?"

At that moment a tall dark skinned woman with long straight black hair in a white bikini and 4 inch heels shimmied up to Ginger saying, "Blowing people's minds again, Ginger?" Then she tilted towards her to whisper into Ginger's ear.

Ginger's face lit up and she returned her focus back to Jake. "Well, Columbia and I have to go take care of some business in the back. Nice talking to you, honey."

"Wait!" Jake blurted out. "I want to be your friend," and turned red as a beet.

Ginger hesitated as she was preparing to leave and turned back to Jake taking his face in her hands as she looked straight into his eyes.

"Did you notice that I talked to you about all the other guys in the club, but I didn't tell you what you were here for?"

Ginger flashed a smile, and sang "Goodbye, little alien!" as she spun away on her heel. Jake watched her and Columbia clip-clop off at a medium trot to the club's curtained back room.

Jake stared off into the space where Ginger's ass had been. He kept staring.

Time passed and the beer in his hand reminded him it was just sitting there getting warm. He lifted the bottle to his lips and pulled on it, though he didn't taste anything.

He thought about what Ginger had said and decided that FantasyLand was palliative care for relationships.

The bachelor party closed down the club.

Jake didn't see Ginger again that night.

* * *

Weeks later, Jake entered the club smiling.

Surveying the floor from the entrance he looked for a face in the crowd.

Unsatisfied, he walked directly to the bar.

"Hey, Nix," Jake addressed the bartender. She came over to greet him with a hug as he stood at the bar. "How are you today? Acid reflux still bothering you?"

"No, I'm good! The apple cider vinegar you told me about really helped. OMG, you totally have to see this video!" She showed Jake a video of a woman getting covered in a giant vat of packing peanuts.

"Oh, shit, that's hilarious." He smiled back at her.

"I know, right? So funny!" With practiced efficiency she tossed a coaster onto the counter in front of Jake, "What can I get you?" She smiled.

Jake asked for a beer and sat on the barstool across from Nix. He folded his arms on the bar.

"Well, I'm looking for Ginger, actually."

"Oh yeah? Well, she's not working tonight. She usually works Tuesday, Thursday and every other weekend. What do you want to see her for?"

"Just to thank her."

"For what?"

Jake leaned on his folded arms, "Last time I was here Ginger opened my eyes to some things about myself that I wasn't willing to take a look at." He paused to consider this. "Guys here talk to the girls because they don't know how to be open and honest with their partners at home. I figure Fantasyland is a way to make up for that gap in their relationships."

Nix placed a can of Budweiser on the coaster in front of Jake and popped the top with her bottle opener.

"I can see that," she nodded.

Jake put money on the bar. It sat there.

"What she said she didn't say about me personally, but I'm a guy here just like any other. I am just as guilty of not communicating with my partners as the rest."

Nix tilted her head slightly to one side and smiled.

"But, there was more to it than that. It went deeper for me. I was using sex as a placeholder for communication for my whole adult life."

Nix brought her eyebrows together, "I'm sorry, I don't follow." She folded her arms across her chest.

"Sex is the most physical intimacy you can have with someone. I was using it as a way to take the place of emotional intimacy. I confused a bond that brings people together emotionally with a physical act. I was just triaging for the void inside my heart." He paused to take a swig of his beer.

"Sure, I hear ya," said Nix, "But what about 'kiss and make up?' We need sex to bridge that gap sometimes. Don't be so hard on yourself, honey."

Jake grinned. "Thanks, Nix, it's all good. I just figured that I didn't want to just be another broken man. I don't want to miss out on the intimacy that comes from being real with someone special. And once I figured that out, don't you know I started seeing someone."

"Good for you," Nix said as she put her hand on Jake's with an encouraging shake.

"Yeah, it has been really great. I feel like I've been more open and trusting with her than I ever have been. It feels really good."

"And how's the sex?" Nix shared a mischievous smile with Jake.

"Best ever!" Jake beamed. They both laughed.

Jake took a pull from his beer, pushed his barstool back, and stood up. "I hate that something as important as intimacy is turned into something you pay for here. But, I figure the best I can do to fight capitalism is to just give my feelings away for free!" He smiled again, "I guess I won't be around much. Tell Ginger when you see her that I said thanks." He reached over the bar and hugged Nix, then walked away and out of the bar.

From the stage Brady watched Jake walk away through the inner doors leading out to the surface of Earth. She spun lazily around her pole. As she danced, she thought about her day job at Target and about what it would take to convince her parents to invest in crypto currency, and Sir Mix-a-Lot played on.

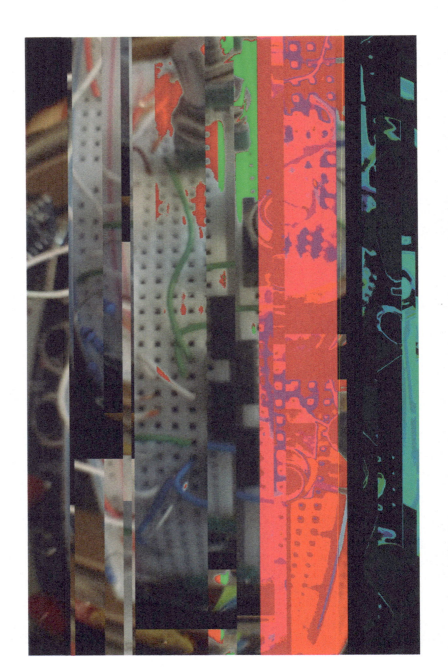

Breach Horizon

PART I: UNITED FRAGMENTS

by Paradox M. Pollack

N.

Epimetheus, the ancient obsidian-skinned Titan, screamed into the black hole from his nautilus shell ship, The Loial. He leaned out beyond the frame of the ledge into the void. The bellows of his voice rumbled the spiral-shaped hull. The scream carried no sound but billowed along the edge of a solar wind that traced a plasma current. The vibration streamed within a million miles of where Earth used to be and exposed a distorted space close to his ship. In this curious bubble, a warp was revealed. Epimetheus stretched out into the vacuum, and with a gentleness that would have impressed a deer, he cupped the distortion and placed it into his pearlescent spacecraft.

"Victory in the final round. That's how humans always played the game. Anything they could get away with, whatever had to be endured, humanity was willing to suffer it. The human story was essentially one long chain of last-round knock-outs as if they were always testing Creation, asking, "are we worth it? What my brother made, by design, was doomed from the start. I suppose that because my children married into humanity, their legacy is mine too. Humans always seemed to clever their way through the maze but delayed at the end so that we could fight the minotaur."

Epi stared into the pair of singularities swirling into each other, an infinity symbol turned inside out, and he pondered his own end.

"Where does consciousness go at the moment of death? All death ends up being the same as every other, from person to civilization to planet. At the completion of a great culture, there is a coiling tide of gravities that sink inward and never stop going down, and that culture never comes out again. A coordinate traverses beyond time and intersects all points in the continuum, no longer a singular expression but one with the singularity."

He looked back at the distortion he had fished from the ether, and it began to take shape.

I.

Greek civilization was dying; it had been under attack for years. The great leaders were corrupted by power, and the powerful were attacked from all sides like a whale carcass by dogs and sand crabs. Spartan and Athenian warfare had eroded the core of Greece. Over its last years, it had staggered between Olympiads, and now its borders crumbled before the Legions of Rome. After this moment, Greece would become a carrion corpse to be stripped of all muscle and sinew, fat and skin, until only bones remained as an armature. An architecture that Rome would empty of its Gods and refill with its own.

Burning incense sticks curled a thick smoke about the room, filling it with the potent scent of myrrh, frankincense, cinnamon, and saffron. Thalia could no longer separate the smells that blanketed her sinus and lungs to suffocation. Her raw throat and tearing eyes were thick with the stale age of stone, and the taste of iron coated her tongue from the dozen goats sacrificed in preparation for this conflict. The sweat of battle, the heated perfume of incense was a deluge of odors, a dense marketplace of sellers all hawking their offerings. Yet, she continued to sing quietly to herself and the Gods, with a blacksmith's hammering focus, as she had for eight hours.

This was the last stand of nine priests and priestesses who had kept the practices and lore from the Eleusinian, Dionysian, and Orphic Mysteries. These sorcerers of the Greek isles had been chased constantly, cornered, and murdered for the last two years like pigs in a stall. Their numbers went from thirty emissaries to twenty-two, diminishing petals of a wilting flower until only these last nine remained. The attack on the temple was imminent, and an understanding between them rang like a lyre's string: This would be the end.

Legionnaires poured into the hall like a flood of mercury, each splattered from the still-wet remains of rulers and peasants alike. Though their swords did not make distinctions, the blood they were about to spill was the purest lines from Greece's ancient priests and priestesses. At the back of the great hall, Thalia watched the warriors pummeling in; they came in wave after wave of heroic passion. It seemed at first that there was a chance, but soon it became clear that those who remained would not be enough to stop the torrent of soldiers.

Sousana of the dreaming host sensed a great wolf had caught their scent, able to stalk their every move. Some elusive ancient magic was being used to track them, and only using the combined skills of the Oracle and Thalia's unique senses of the future had they evaded quick annihilation, but it seemed a string had already been curled in a loop and placed through the hole, it was only a matter of time before the knot was pulled tight.

Under the official temple and through the secret door, Thalia had followed her vision and chose to hide here behind the battlements intended to defend from this kind of attack. Thalia stood on the marble dias at the back of the great hall dredged and shaped by the workers and artisans of Corinth. Of the remaining Keepers, Thalia was the weakest for killing, but she carried a talent, a deep and secret thread that went back through the ages of the Delphic Oracles. She could see time as her precise position and navigate with a compass that directed her to where she had to be within the landscape of time. These visions came as flashes and a gentle or tense pulling in the direction from inside. There was no pulling now. Only a sense of being planted here like a long-forgotten forest temple tree. Her feet were rooted in this place, her mind embracing the endlessness of time.

Thalia cast her prayers into the dense currents of the fire's smoke, herbs, and air, blood, and sweat in the atmosphere, subtle winds in the stale underground, and she called upon the oldest of gods to hear her: The smoke billowed and quivered in rhythm with her song.

'While you live,
Shine in Delight
life exists only for a short while,
and time demands its toll.'

It was a humble song, vibrating in her pipes like a small bird's warbling, but it called upon the oldest forces from before even the birth of Night, Erebus, Tartarus, or Kronos. It was a call to and from the beginning of the unformed. The song revealed the limited and delicate way that one life of flesh and bone, heart and dreams, could understand the chaos we come from and to which we return. Thalia had chanted her hymn for what seemed an eternity, going deeper into its mysteries.

The song's tones gave strength to her kinsmen. As she sang, it revealed the fates' threads as a silken milk-like fabric suspended across all things in her visual field. As she prepared her spell components, she remembered each offering to her as a puzzle. It seemed that some strange destiny slowly formed from the gifts of her allies, and it all came to this moment as the final piece was laid into place.

The Maenad, Oenone, had given Thalia the Thessalian whip. She carried it with her for three years and soaked it daily, from handle to fall, in oils and distilled components of each of the ancient holy gods. Thalia winced at the memory of Oenone's death. The Maenad would swirl a host inside her as the madness took her; she could sustain every damage without injury by precise and fevered animal violence. She became the damage, defused it out of space, and made each attack against her useless. However, eventually, the enemy found her weakness. The vision of a shoreline filled with blood was muddied with rage in Thalia's memory as she honored her, "A true sacrifice which saved all who remain."

The priest of Saturnus had given her the paint, a resin refined from a black feather fossil of the First Raven mixed with holy water. Over the last nine months, she prepared her whip by drawing lines across its length in preparation for precisely this moment. Toward its end the whip got thinner and thinner, and the lines painted closer and closer together. Today, she was finally painting the end of the whip that cracks.

The whip's cracker was made from one hundred hairs of a centaur's tail. These hairs had been drawn from Chiron's father before his horse-man body burned on its funeral pyre. Kerberos of Crete had given her those centaur tail hairs when they met for the first time years ago. Kerberos was a Priest of Iapetus, the father of Titans, carrying an almost forgotten legacy of rituals from the dawn of man. He and Thalia had been lovers in exile, sharing force and tenderness as an inhale and exhale. So she sang, sucking in her tears as she watched Kerberos, only a few body lengths away, crushed against the wall by blow after blow of the Roman centurions. His great strength and endurance, trained from years of intentional agony, began to form cracks, and his pride in his prowess let a stray iron get through. At the last, before his skull caved, he shot a glance across the chaos of combat and caught her eyes. Then he was gone, submerged in the currents of fury.

The Imperial force's weapons had been enchanted so that Olympian magic would not touch them. Only here in this place of power was there any hope of survival. She looked over the carnage as it continued to edge closer to where she sang. Yet, as she viewed the combat, it seemed too slow. She could see through the visible world and the puppet strings above the enemy. A new power supported the Legionnaires; their steel and iron armor and blades seemed immune to the whispers and thunders of the Greek Gods. There were thousands of Roman Legionnaires blessed in this way, and they just kept coming.

With each of her fellow's deaths, a piece of her left this world. The edge of the steel blade, curved circumference of the mace, point of an arrow or spear each found their mark. Two hundred Spartan warriors were assigned to defend the alliance of priests, and yet each battle dwindled their number to the final ninety of the greatest warriors. Each of their life's delicate bubbles burst, and they went down. Thalia thought, "In the Roman's minds, they are the heroes building a new world. It is crushing to feel that a blessing for one side of a war is a curse for the other."

Thalia anointed the end of the hairs with a mixture of mercury and a thick dark resin. This resin was what the Priestess of Morpheus called "the last drops from Uranus' loins, the same dark and vibrant seed that formed Aphrodite from sea foam before even Hestia was born."

The priestess of Morpheus, Sousana of Thasos, fell as Thalia drew the syrup droplets across the hairs of the whip. Susana's head separated from her body while holding 50 of the barbarians in thrall with a tale of autumn leaves. The barbarians who had been stopped by her story were weeping madly. Eventually, they would die of dehydration, moaning and scraping the dirt with grief until they sobbed their last breath. Thalia thought, "At least some of our magic is still able to breach their defenses."

Having completed her preparation and approaching the end of a cycle of 888 repetitions of the psalm, Thalia took a breath and held it. The last notes of the melody rang across every surface, toning a new shape of time that she sensed stretching farther than she had ever imagined. She could feel the tracing of the fingers of the Fates resonating the strings of time in a symphony.

From silence and stillness, Thalia lifted the whip's handle to her shoulder. She paused for a moment after years of disciplined searching for the center of the moment, and Thalia made a perfect figure eight in front of her body by turning her arm and wrist in rapid and precise synchrony from her elbow.

She sent two loops down the length of the whip's leather, which resounded thunderously each time they reached the end of the loop. Faster than the speed of sound, the whip crack sprayed mercury off its end to her left and right, splattering the far walls, the ceiling, and the floor before her in a perfect circle.

Her voice pronounced her phrasing of the oldest hymn. It had built a flood of energy from inside her.

"... *Shine* ..."

Standing before her months ago, with volcanic smoke and prepared herbs, uniting them into a singular consciousness, the nameless oracle of Delphi moved her hand the same as a trainer of athletes, showing her the precise way to bring her mind to a single point and the swift and exact double strike to break the fabric of time.

Though this magic had never before been enacted, it worked perfectly. It reached the ears of the Gods and beyond.

"... *In* ..."

As the sound rang through the great hall, she could feel the ripple of the whip-crack, a gust of wind through a forest fire.

"... *Delight* ..."

Smoke and fire merged, thread and fabric, life and thought pulled apart at the seams. Her form extended through the eye of a needle and light through a prism. The smoke of her human life blew out of the way, and she could feel the fire of Prometheus' gift tear through the cloth of Fate's tapestries.

Time was no longer pulse by pulse but a singular source that stretched from the falling rain in the mountain streams to the ocean currents and then back again by the evaporating heat of the sun, creating clouds.

Everything became still except the sound of tearing fabric, not the fabric of fibers but the fabric of sound itself. For the first time in her life, she knew the Gods were listening and willing to respond.

The whip crack's rippled out beyond the deep cavern below Corinth, distorting time the way soundwaves distort the air. Thalia came undone, and her body ascended with the ghosts of the Greek gods' priests like a dolphin in a pod. All those newly murdered in the name of Rome rose up to rage with her.

The warp of the crack echoed back into the past and passed the last Olympiads. The cheers for champions merged with the cries for mercy and the howls of death. For history, it was sunset, Corinth 146 BC, and for the timeless ones, it was whip-o-clock as she made the leap from the fourth to the fifth dimension.

When time's dimension is traversed, there is a period of adjustment that cannot be called evolution.

There is only one moment in forever.

Consciousness, however, has an orgasm and wants to create everything at once.

Thalia's being was vibrated apart by familiar things; her pulse, her breath, her tiny motions that resisted gravity as she walked or stood. These things shattered her.

She became a cloud of atomized living energy/matter that shifted shapes as the cloud followed her imagination into numerous forms. What were once organs became satellites outside Thalia's body, and her womb made worlds that expanded and flourished and then turned to ash as she watched countless times. Each time, novel creatures, entirely unique but adjacent to her own form, would build civilizations and die in war, disease, and hunger, bat-faced, hundred-limbed, winged, and chitin skinned. They swelled and diminished, rotted and regrew as she coiled in on herself, unable to do anything but watch. Her life became meaningless. All she had fought for over the last three years against the Legions of Rome was forgotten. In a pressure current of instant depth, she merged with the Muse for whom she was named. She was the hinges at the corners of the doorframe of life and the door of time slammed shut.

II.

Epimetheus was posting live to his Akashic signal stream, and although most of his audience had already heard the schtick, there were an unusual number of listeners to this Versal soul-cast, upward of a few trillion beings from a couple dozen planets.

"The human model was a successful fabrication, yet I immediately saw the flaws. My brother Prometheus and I had many conversations about the qualities of his clay creations. What should they be like? What would they need? He didn't want my input, but I advised him anyway. I could see how they were going to end. It is the curse of looking ever backward. As you know, I can look back from any point in time." He howled, raising his voice to the volume of thunder, "The past and the future mean nothing to me."

Everyone listening knew the score.

Epi was a Versal streaming celebrity, the last of his kind and the final remainder of a dead race. He paused for effect and to take in the reality of what he was saying, "Except at this moment. This is the moment where I cannot look back." He continued at a quicker pace, beginning to feel the musical quality of his voice and taking the audience on a journey.

"No Titans are left to take responsibility for what humanity did to the galaxy. Prometheus, or as we liked to call him, "Meth," created an audience for his tragedies. Prometheus is celebrated and remembered for his sacrifice and redemptions amidst his many dramas. Shaping humanity from clay, stealing fire from the Gods, and his punishment of having his liver taken from his body every day. We could see this moment from different perspectives, the end of us all. As an equalization, he made me promise to take this final judgment on my shoulders at the edge of the Blaedensae's domain."

Epimetheus flexed his invisible selves, the energy bodies that carried his Titan-level powers, and the Versal audience flushed with a radiant rush of presence. This rush is the main reason people showed up for his broadcasts. Every time Epi opened his Akashic channel, you would get the Epi Flex at some point.

For many Versal episodes, Epi hinted about journeying to the universal center carrying the weight of his immense history. As Epi was the only one to survive a cosmic catastrophe, he had come here to the center of the universe to have a final audience with the oldest of his kin. They were the last remaining children of Chaos.

"Before the Blaed arrive, I have called a friend to be my witness across time. This is not my story to tell, but hers and hers alone."

Epimetheus had been hinting about this "special guest" forever, a kind of magic trick he was going to pull out of his hat for his final performance. His audience had grown to expect this kind of spectacle from him.

"Some of you understand through your extensions of thought that consciousness is infinite, but the building blocks of life are not. Whether silicon, carbon, or nitrogen-based, you are guided almost entirely by the fabric your consciousness threaded through.

"Great sacrifice requires an understanding of why you sacrifice." He reached down, lifted the distortion, and made his way through the pearl, gold, and precious stone base-relief sculptures. The sculptures lined the walls, illustrating erotic enactments in an intricate style.

"No one remembers the power of sacrifice. At the end of life, a being will always ask themselves this question. How will I stare into the center of infinity and not go mad? How will I become one with the singularity and not lose myself? What is it to become one with the void? I don't know your answer, but many of you will remember my advice from my best-viewed Versal, "23 Steps to Being Immortal."

"#2 Take responsibility for everything.

#3 You accomplish what life wants for you with good friends and everyday luck.

Find luck in every crease, crevice, and niche, and put it in your pocket because you will need it.

12 Call upon your friends often and always be grateful.

#20 Return the favor.

#23 Know when to stop."

Epi had remained on course with his faster-than-imagination ship and spent the last centuries traveling to the center of the universe. As a showman, Epi worked the audience; the buildup and suspense were killing them. It had been lifetimes for some listeners, and some planets had to pass on the lore from generation to generation. It all led to this final event, and so here, with the mic in his hand, and because his audience had been dwindling and he was drunk on his own ego, Epimetheus got sloppy enough, to tell the truth. That is how full transparency in the universe began. Unfortunately, it's also how his career ended.

III.

Undone. You are coming undone.

The seams of self are split. Phases of tension and release hammer you with nails at perfect angles. This fury of action around you constructs a design. It reveals to you the blueprint of a hidden world beyond creation. Amid the flames which gravity shapes, you became the explosion of the first sun and united with the roots of the Abyss.

Not one of us wants to exist, nor do we wish to cease existing once we start, and from there, the battle begins. Yet, remembering at the beginning of endlessness calls us back again to time.

We barely remember this moment of return, a partial view that becomes longing. A house of many images and metaphors, training and tendencies, frames of meaning from before understanding, and these fragments compose trajectories, facing different directions, and unify through a confrontation of resistances.

Thalia moved through the universe no longer in a linear fashion, but by punching holes through realities and dancing for moments in each of the worlds she occupied.

In this opening and reaching and closing, she was stabbed, brought to a hospital four hundred years later, and found herself in and out of libraries, bank vaults, over canyons, and inside rivers. Each time she found herself in a new place, she would reach for a luminescent object whose glow would appear in her presence. This way, she secured a few items through her travels that would help her in her future adventures.

Watching her life and the lives of those that birthed from her, she pondered the reality of the Gods. The skin of the Gods were all scars from the turbulence they had survived. For the aches and pains that one human can acquire, imagine then the breadth of a life that has lived as long as the Earth itself, billions of years.

There was a distortion that pulled and pressed her through it. All the life she had mothered became a moth and flame heading toward each other, Thalia's point of entry back into time.

IV.

"My brother always got his way." Epimetheus paced with strides of a mountain across the iridescent pearl floor of The Loial.

"Our mythology gets echoed down to the mortal world. A thousand lifetimes of whispers were written and rewritten to serve each person who lived. Just like Meth, every household and king changed the plot to serve themselves, but just the same, I'll set the record straight before I end my life and my tale."

Epi took a mighty swig of a distillation harvested from a giant gas planet. The flagon, composed of alloy gold and adamantine, shimmered from the potency of its contents. As the liquid danced down his throat to his organs, he flushed seven shades darker than his already obsidian complexion, and a shudder ran through his perfect form. His body came unhinged, swiftly reacting to the power coursing through him. He shut the cap sculpted from a compressed white dwarf star. With his Titan's strength, he struggled for a moment and then achieved the seal to retain the fermented planet's freshness. The harvested armageddon hissed in his skull, and he laughed, a terrible laugh of delirium that rippled out across the empty space as his eyes settled on the goal of his journey for the first time, a pit of densest darkness where two black holes were swirling.

Epimetheus trembled there as the fermentation of a planet coursed his veins. He was in every way the perfect embodiment of the form that creation designed. Humans were merely an echo of the measured beauty of his muscle curves and bone's broad shoulders.

Epi's face twisted up in anger and sadness, nostalgia and regret.

"My brother, the martyr, the saint, the hero, HA!. Everyone looked to him as a bright and shining star, but he was merely ahead of the curve. He was made that way, stubborn, and always right even when he was obviously wrong. They are all gone now, swept away. No one left, just me."

Epimetheus realized he had drunkenly fallen forward over the edge of his ship's helm, a thin wire frame shaped from the iron in the blood of Cyclops. The guidance system of his ship, The Loial, was an astounding technology wherein whatever one thought became instantly visualized and could be navigated. The navigation system calculated something massive with a billion shimmers organized and exchanging infrared and ultraviolet colors between nodes, a painting of fluctuating maths that describes math.

This ship and its magical helm were a gift from Hephaestus some generations ago when Epi started soul-casting about how he had been epically screwed by the Gods. Hephe felt guilty, so he made Epi a ship guided by pure imagination that could move between the infinite bleeds of existence.

Epi wailed, "I didn't choose this destination. It was an oath. It was an oath I made to Pandora."

Epi prided himself on his tragedy after he lost his wife. Hephaestus, who understood the tragedy of love, having been married to Aphrodite during the shaping of the universe, was more than sympathetic and had worked hard to make a gift worthy of Epi's loss.

Hephe had crafted this vessel, a spiral shell ship that was now close enough to harness the exterior tentacles of gravity from a black hole. The ship's engine used these forces as a power source to transmit Epi's broadcast across dimensions.

As Thalia arrived, Epi turned his attention to the bubble distortion, which became the consciousness of the one human left in the universe, the last of her kind, which he pulled from her stasis between dimensions.

Epi stitched a cynical smile at the edge of his lips and spoke directly to Thalia, whose screaming eternity had started to reform as her body-in-time on his ship. Now she gazed at him as he towered in his space castle made of iridescent pearl.

Wild perspective careened at her as he brought his head close to hers.

"There is a gateway behind Io, and you cracked your whip at exactly the right instant to be welcome-wormed through time. As humanity is the measure of all things, and you had the same spark and clay of divinity, you made your way. Of course, I called you here too, but you had to wish it."

For the Versal viewer, Epi was a giant with prismatic shadows radiating from him at the center of a fractal. Epimetheus spoke into a nautilus shell-shaped microphone, sculpted into a nautilus-shaped room at the center of a nautilus-shaped hull which carried him through space and sent Versals out into the great expanse. A snake of the golden mean, a coiled spiral ship eating the tail of its endlessly receding derivative remainders.

Information pooled in the crevices surrounding his body, perceptions and thoughts expressed simultaneously on multiple dimensions.

The viewers could feel the consciousness he was sharing as a nesting mother to her young, hungry baby birds. Thalia toyed with this nourishment like a bead on a string. She could draw time back and forth across his words. An ineffable feeling of being chosen blossomed in her heart as Epi smiled from behind his bones at her.

For Thalia, as he spoke, the sound of his voice became long strings that curled into Moebius springs that coiled around the meaning of his words and whipped vibration together with intention. Each word is a resounding loop to the source of creation and back again.

Thalia saw the whole message from beginning to end. Looking at the breadth of his entire life, she wanted to weep, but she could only laugh.

Epimetheus' form was free from the imposed actions-of-matter-as-extension-of-mind; his being was the entire evolution of a singular object.

To navigate this, imagine the piano's development from the first moment of human fascination focused upon a resonating plant fiber twine. Now imagine all the stages of string; first, the guts of an animal, then thin resonant metal, eventually becoming the architectural wonder of resonance that is the body of the piano. The composer's work practices the technique of ten fingers upon this delicate machine and finally congeals a composition formulated and forged into a final form and then played throughout the universe repeatedly, slowly refining. The layers in a Liszt or Beethoven composition are suspended in a fermenting fluid, steeped in technique practiced for each iteration and interaction. Every gesture of Epimetheus became an ancient understanding, within the timing of a pulse from the heart to fingertip. This eternity in time would have been astounding if it had not always been so. Already six hundred million years of this ever-present genius of Creation's form and function.

"I'm sorry little one. It must be a bit disorienting here. Let me take you on my shoulder for a moment to see what is happening."

Time slowly became stable. The edges of forms became more precise and the layers of objects retained their skins and structures. Light no longer passed through things to reveal their trajectory of creation through negation; their "all-time at once-ness." Now, life and matter and energy held their forms, and the lines of their shapes exposed their fleeting lightness and density of being, revealing Nature moment to moment again and again.

The glittering stars drew her eye, and each seemed to have its own pulsing density and distance. Thalia began to sense which orbits were close and which were far, which of them had great size and which were small dust nodes. blade

It was all more than her mind could manage, so Epimetheus again held her delicately, a blade of grass between his fingers, a fragile bubble he did not want to burst. The fullness of his power, his gravitational density, and the great consequence that poured from his eyes became her own strength. With his thoughts, he turned her line of sight to where he was looking.

There, the double swirl of the singularities merging took in their perception, and she could feel a horrible intelligence speeding back at her. Somehow, she altered her awareness to avoid the regard of this ancient gaze. A flood of feelings occurred, which coursed its power within her.

She could feel the support of Epimetheus' powers inside her though she didn't know how to use them.

Her most subtle movements were flames, the sun rays directing time to move in one direction and the other. When she took a deep inhale, she could feel the stretch back to before planets and then exhale to the extraordinary vision of ornate boats launching into the stars sending lances of light across the magnet of space to tear the carbon black skin of their hulls, pouring sailors out into the dark.

Thalia still dazed from her journey, wondered why a Titan had scooped her out of her life's dream. She wondered if the spell she cast and the whip she cracked, still dangling from her hand, was intended for strictly this transport beyond the river Styx and the boundary of Oceanus to the Erebus, the night that housed the constellation of stars. Nothing but a vast swirl of darkness. Thalia's eyes reflected the incessant night; she remembered then the absence of light that her eyes took in as they formed in her mother's womb.

When she stopped playing with this new capacity, the swirl and curl of time righted itself again, and she could see the actual breadth and flash of consciousness as it vibrated the vitreous fluids interrupting, augmenting, and stretching the flow of time.

"You could not have been prepared for this," he whispered, speaking to her as if she was the only audience of his words. "From the moment that Prometheus sculpted you, I knew all of Olympus' traditions would fail, and Gaea's instinct would no longer bring you to your knees. You could have only ever leaped toward this vertigo of merging singularities. Time is catching up to you, little clay baby. Your whole lineage has been hypnotized by your consciousness, dazzled by the infinite force that lived in your finite form." The pulse from the center of the singularities seemed to notice them now. Thalia became scared, and Epimetheus changed his pitch from a father who criticizes to a friend who comforts.

"The edge of reality has come back to bite you, and no longer can you return to the innocence of animals. No longer will simple similes and metaphors help bind you to the cadence of experience which integrates meaning. It is why nothing could ever make sense to your kind again. Once you made the progression to language and stood at the edge of imagination's Abyss, you began to confront Nature's instinct. The wider the split, the further into Delirium your race traveled. I would have wept for you, but it has been my curse to know how you would end as soon as you were born."

V.

Thalia was tracking his tale as Epimetheus spoke:

"Take my wife, please."

Epi's face twisted into a mixture of rage, bitterness, and sorrow while a laugh track as part of his Versal soul cast resounded through the ship.

"My brother looked forward and pressed the flesh to get his own way, you see. Handshakes and smiles to get a result. He had his campaigns, got the rewards, paid the price, made the sacrifices, yadda, yadda, yadda."

She took in the vastness of the Titan's voice, but the bitterness in the tone did not match the wonder in his eyes.

The vertigo of measuring relationships of scale dizzied Thalia.

The difference between their dimensions was a mouse and a mountain, a whale and a snail. This, Thalia could measure, but the twin black holes before them, the breadth of the expansive view, this she could still not manage, even with the Titan's assistance.

She thought to herself, still unable to use her mouth for words." Chaos lived before creation. The source of Tartarus kept all of Epimetheus' kin, a radiant light, trapped inside this Abyss. The source of this dark Abyss comes forward as a hungry wave reaching toward a shore and drawing everything into its undertow.

This wave, this pulse, seems to arrive more and more frequently as Epimetheus speaks to me. I feel it the same as I knew my mother's voice as I grew in her womb. Then, finally, all of these memories became easy for me to reach."

An emptiness that receives and calibrates all of the connections of the soul to its habitat. A camera captures light on the back of the chamber, and the eye registers light on the retina. All probable chains of actions and possible choices are written by fibers, not simply a skin; it is more the algae dense in the ocean where each part is individually absorbing, suspended in the water, undulating with the waves of possibility. All intentions are registered; variations of emotion and valence of opportunities bring the components together into a whole.

"When Zeus asked my brother to make worshipers, of all the options and possibilities, he made matter curl in on itself, and they become little versions of himself. That was humanity." Epimetheus emphasized the past tense, broadcasting to Thalia that there had already been an ending. He continued with a biting annunciation, "Calling him a narcissist is like calling the universe big. It goes without saying and doesn't even come close to expressing what you mean.

"So I'll tell the story that has been told millions of times in the central chamber of initiation where children become men and women." As he took a breath to begin, Thalia saw an ocean of moments between children and adults across creation.

"It begins with Chaos.

Birth of night, dark, and the underworld. All the first children of nothing, including the birds and love. Creation stories were how human society fetched the ancestors to reveal their understanding. My family and our roots were no different. Before she died, my daughter and I spoke of humanity; we acknowledged that a flood was not enough to erase the human signal then and would not be enough now. Whoever survives will partner with forces from before the Gods. The essence of Chaos before the birth of love. To do that, they will have to be erased to find their true purpose." It is here in this crucible that your kind learned the way forward. How to be a person in the crowd without disappearing but by becoming responsible. How to assert oneself without needing to control. This method of shaping human ways worked for a time but became distorted.

The telling changed. No more was it the birds and love that were the source of creation, but each force was vying for the center ring, the ring of power and control. Humanity was to fight for that ring to the very end, and at this loss, being a sore loser, they took the entire galaxy with them.

The memories of his daughter became so intense that she began to appear. Pyrrha is on the soul cast, and the soul cast swiftly registers an outpouring of love for Epi's daughter. The listeners are suddenly full of the feeling of seeing their ex-wife when they have a child with someone else.

"The Blaed's purpose is to harvest each Fate of humanity, and now that none are answerable but me, I have come to face my responsibility. The Bladensae are content to dance in their awareness at the edges of the universal planes, skirting along Tartarus and Olympus, Elysium and Hell, but they were once, a long time ago, called from the cloud and vapor, vacuum and storm to settle a dispute between two gods.

As I'm sure you know, Apollo and Dionysis, older and younger gods, were entrained in controversy about the Nature of the universe and which one of them served the universe more. Their worshipers had been warring in the realms of Delirium, whose power was fresh from her transformation. The worshipers of Apollo were so hungry for the light that, like Icarus, they destroyed not only their minds and wings but tore the fiber and burned the skin of all the animals to understand them, to dig beneath their flesh for the codes of life itself. The Dionysians were in an ecstatic trance that consumed whole nations. In the face of that drought, they created an oasis. They sought the inner world as their domain and left the world behind.

The original Titans watched these young Gods from behind the veil of their prison in Tartarus and sent a message through my brother Prometheus.

They signaled him with rumbles below the Earth. This was after he shaped humankind but before stealing fire. My wife, Pandora, was fabricated as a temptation to me and a betrayal of humanity. The evils that she released upon society were a trick of the Gods. This was long ago. The Blaedensae were called to judge a winner between humans and the gods.

Who was making the most progress toward finding the true Nature of creation? They challenged the Erinyes. I brought myself all the way to the home of the Blaedensae for a reason. You will be immune to their powers; I made sure of that. As I do battle with them for the death of my wife and child, I will tell you the tale of all that was so that you may keep it and bring it with you into this new universe."

His head bowed as if at a funeral, and he seemed to resolve himself.

"The fates are personified by their desire to get rid of the Titans. Each Titan had a gift. My brother got the glowing flame that everyone looked to in awe and inspiration that could breathe life into the inanimate, and I got this pocket universe at the end of everything. Meth's desire to erase me from history made it possible to have this little pocket outside of time.'

He turned to Thalia. "I just called you to witness my victory."

She looked down and saw the pearl floor absorb her shadow and reflection. All radiances, dark and light, digested energy's emanation and matter's richness into the ship's refracting material. Thalia knew that Epimetheus' words were a joke. There would be no victory, just a sacrifice to sustain her beyond his end.

FRANKFORD PUBLISHING
TOP 10 SCIENCE FICTION BOOKS OF ALL-TIME

1. DUNE (1965)
by Frank Herbert

2. FRANKENSTEIN (1818)
by Mary Shelley

3. BRAVE NEW WORLD (1932)
by Aldous Huxley

4. NINETEEN EIGHTY-FOUR (1949)
by George Orwell

5. DHALGREN (1975)
by Samuel R. Delaney

6. THE LEFT HAND OF DARKNESS (1969)
by Ursula K. LeGuin

7. KINDRED (1979)
by Octavia Butler

8. NEUROMANCER (1984)
by William Gibson

9. DO ANDROIDS DREAM OF ELECTRIC SLEEP? (1968)
by Phillip K. Dick

10. I AM LEGEND (1954)
by Richard Matheson

"Sunrise in Brooklyn", by Jackrabbit

PART II: THE VISIBLE SPECTRUM

A Walk Through Greenpoint

by Jackrabbit

The black box.

Your mind.

It is a black box.

You do not know what is going on inside of it. You have no idea how it operates. Why do you do the things that you do? You have no idea. You do them. You just do them and you hope the story you invent after the fact makes enough sense to get you through to another day.

***

This story you invent starts with you sitting on your wife's bed.

You notice something on her white duvet cover and you mention it to her, raising your voice enough so she can hear you in the other room.

"Oh, that's just ice cream," she walks in and sits down at her desk as she answers you. "Maya and I got a pint from this artisanal place around the corner. Must have dripped while I was eating in bed. I'm overdue for a laundry day anyway." She talks without looking at you, focused instead on whatever she's typing on her phone. "Thanks for pointing it out." She types fast.

Of course it is ice cream. You must be crazy to think that ice cream looks like cum stains. Your stare gets lost in the small organically irregular ovals of light grey that gradate out to a yellowish border.

But it is so hard for you not to think of her with another man. Another man is why you're here now in Greenpoint after she left you 3,000 miles behind in San Francisco.

Heart racing and blood filling your ears you ignore the flush that burns your cheeks. Be the person you think she always wanted you to be. Suck it up. Push the fear down. Be the person you never could be till it was too late.

A change of pace might be good for you. "I'm getting a glass of water, you want anything while I'm up?" You ask as you walk to the door of her bedroom.

She shakes her head without looking up. From where you are in the doorway it looks like she's on social media.

You turn into the shared space of the apartment. It's pretty sizable compared to Manhattan. You don't notice anything about it, though. You're too busy trying to figure out what she's thinking. How do you make yourself more appealing? What do you say next?

What she's thinking is that she left you. She's thinking that you wasted the chance to be her man when you had your opportunity. Once she was gone the time you'd squandered with her became the most precious moments of your life. Your goal became panning for more of those moments at any cost. Any foothold into her heart—does that make it a hearthold?—needs to be sought after and amplified if you are going to win her back. That's the strategy.

You notice her roommate sitting at the table on the far side of the common space.

"Hi, Maya. You're up late," as you walk past her to the sink.

She looks up long enough from her bowl of chocolate ice cream to share an emotionless smile.

It seems likely to you that she's privy to every sordid scintilla of your personal life.

Penelope had introduced you to Maya for the first time earlier in the day. You just met her so there is little else to say. Like Penelope, she's a cute-Asian-hipster girl. Like Penelope, she is happy to ignore you.

Next to the sink you find a glass and push the spigot handle back. You hold the glass under the spout—a vintage Welch's jelly jar with Betty and Veronica from Archie comics throwing a party.

You're thinking about the trolley track that ran down California street in San Francisco. You and Penelope lived there at the border of Nob Hill and the Tenderloin. You would smile when you called it the Tender Knob.

At the corner store you had political conversations with the guy who ran the register, an Iraqi who fought against Saddam in the 90s. There was an Indian restaurant across the street. It was clear the owners weren't cultivating White patrons considering how spicy the food was. The cooks left whole cloves and cardamom pods floating in their concoctions, flavor grenades for the unwary diner.

You return to her room and close the door behind you. Penelope is lying on her back on the bed. She's got her eyes closed. You can hear the song she's listening to. It's Edward Sharpe and the Magnetic Zeros' "Home." After she left you, this was the song you posted to social media in the hopes its simple message would signal to her that your change of heart was sincere.

"Holy Moley me oh my you're the apple of my eye! Girl I never loved one like you!"

Penelope opens her eyes and sees you staring at her.

Her brow furrows. The corners of her mouth flex slightly downward.

This is an intimate moment, this is a spot where you can show her how much you want her. How passionate you can be with her. You move towards her; lips forward eyes locked on her lips.

As she moves away a few degrees while raising her hand between the two of you, she states, "I'm listening to this because I want to think back to the time when we were happy together."

"I want that, too," you talk over her last word.

"But, I can't think of anything. I know there was a time."

"Like when we walked the trail to Tennessee Valley Beach!" Your eagerness stepping on her words.

"But I don't feel that time. I know it was there, but I don't feel it. I can't deny that you've been good to me since I've been here in New York. You've helped make the transition here easier for me."

"I love you, I want to make it all up to you."

"I know you do, but I have to find my own way here now."

"I want to be with you the way you always wanted me to be, though." You're sure the desperation leaks through your words, but it's hard to feign confidence right now, to project an aura of patience and acceptance. Her words are stirring up a cyclone of anxiety. "I'm doing the things you always wanted."

"I know baby, but it is a different situation now." You can tell she's trying. She's making an effort. She cares about you! She hasn't given up on the two of you. You're sure of it. You do your best to shut out the stories she told you about kissing someone in McCarren Park after picking them up at Union Pool. Fucking meat market. Hipster kids working at Vice or some start up in Dumbo decked out in the vintage crap they picked up at Buffalo Exchange. Jesus fucking Christ, how hard is it to go thrift shopping at the Salvation Army? The 70s were fucking stupid, why are you trying to look like that is where you're from? Dear Lord you hate them. And you hate that Penelope wants to be one of them. "What is there to go back to? I put up with it for as long as I could, now I need to be myself."

The fear was overwhelming, but there was no telling if this was going to be your only chance to make your case, "Once we moved in together I realized I had been wrong all that time. I love you. I want you. I am going to make it up to you if you just let me." You reach for her to show her that you want her now. The passion she always wanted to feel from you was right here for her to take.

Penelope puts her hand on your chest retarding your gesture towards her. There is a look of reproach tinged with pity in her eyes. "Where was this when you were fucking those other women?"

"I regret it every day." Your head is spinning. Your skin is hot. You are standing on a sand pile at the edge of a deep black pit. "But, I'm here now and I want you now and I'm the person you always wanted me to be."

"I never wanted to hurt you. But I don't want to be married to you anymore. I'm not trying to push you away. It's your choice to be here. But, I can't commit to being with you."

This isn't the first time you've heard this from her. But, that doesn't seem to matter behind your eyes. The sand moves so that your feet can't find any way to keep you from the edge. The pit you're standing in front of opens its pitch black arms to encircle you as you fall into cold despair. Though inches away from the woman you love, you're completely alone in an uncaring world.

You feel seconds away from collapsing into a heap of skin and hair, emptied of all substance—a simulacrum of yourself filled with just enough air to keep speaking. At that moment she excuses herself to go to the bathroom.

You're grateful to have a second to rally.

You can do this. It's going great. Just keep focused on...

Her phone lights up sitting there on the bed where she left it. It makes the noise of an incoming text.

You wonder who is texting her at 2am so you reach for the phone.

The world is a story.

There are no rules.

There is no foundation.

It is all just a series of meanings we impose on top of the information our senses provide.

What is the story you tell yourself when you pick up the phone to read, "You want me to come over?"

It's from "Chad 'Aleksandr'".

Where do our stories come from? The black box.

The icey cold pit of loss you were falling through turns into a cyclone fire tunnel of hatred.

This FUCKER!

This horny piece of GARBAGE!

Jitbag hipster looking to get his dick wet with a late night booty call.

Without being aware you're doing it, your fingers fly across the phone's keyboard. First, you unlock the phone with its passcode—the one you spied over Penelope's shoulder earlier in case you might need it.

Then you respond to Chad "Aleksandr."

"Come over so I can kick this shit out of you, asshole. Never text my wife again!"

There's nothing satisfying about the action. It's done on autopilot, a lizard response from your brain stem resulting in a sent text.

Penelope walks into the room just as you hit send.

"What are you doing with my phone?" Her brows knit together, but there is a touch of fear in her voice as she realizes what is happening.

"Fuck! I told him not to text me tonight!" She exhales and whisks the phone from your hands. Her eyes widen, "What did you do?"

"Why would you invite me up here if this is what is going on?" The fury evoked by her lover's text started to dissipate as soon as you hit the send button and now the feeling of falling is returning.

Shame and embarrassment rise like bile to the back of your teeth.

Penelope's black eyebrows lift as she texts damage control on her phone. She doesn't notice you grabbing your things as you shove them into your backpack. "What did you do?" She whines again.

As you zip up the bag, a thought comes to you and you straighten up, "Aleksandr?" You're incredulous. "The Mikhail Baryshnikov character from Sex in the City? Jesus fucking Christ."

Her face relaxes slightly, "I didn't think you paid any attention to that show," her voice softer.

"I fucking hated it. But when didn't you have it playing on the TV?" Resentment elbows shame and embarrassment out of the way long enough for you to get angry again. "A bunch of ruling class white women living their best life in New York?" You pause long enough to contort your face into a look of disgust and finish with, "You're welcome to it."

You storm out of her room towards the door to the apartment. "Where are you going?" She calls after you as she gets up to follow. "It's the middle of the night, there are no trains or buses."

Now you're being led by a red devil urging you on—demanding that you move your feet forward. Behind you egging you on is a green devil laughing at you while calling you things like "pencil dick" and "cuckold". Good thing they're there. Without their motivations you wouldn't be able to find the door at all. You're disoriented. Why are the feet moving? Where are they taking you?

Doesn't matter. Just have to go there. Just have to move to move away from this shame away from this disgust. This confusion. Are you angry? Are you doing this out of self preservation? Or is this just a way for you to perversely accommodate her. Is this you getting out of her way so she can have her ice cream? Her late night fuck. Her hipster stud.

This is what she felt for years. The shame, the embarrassment, the disgust.

As you fumble with the door she's standing next to you. Saying she's sorry you had to see that and she didn't mean for it to happen like this.

A moment of clarity washes over you and you use the moment to respond.

"I should have never come here. I can't believe that you would welcome me here knowing how this would make me feel. I know, I deserve it. I regret how I treated you. But this hurts." You reach for the door handle. "I'm never going to see you again."

With that you rush out of the door and close it behind you before you change your mind.

* * *

Every step feels like it is taking you miles away from her. As you walk down the stairs to the building exit you feel as though you're descending deeper into the darkness of alienation and solitude.

You push through the door. Outside the world is silent. You thought New York was always awake. Where is everyone? It's quiet. No one is around. It is just you and the rest of the trash under the streetlights.

You head down to Greenpoint Avenue and make a left.

You really have no idea where you are or what you're doing. All you know is you have to keep moving. Get to the bus and get back home.

A sign on a red building catches your eye: "LIVE POULTRY Slaughter" flatly stares out at you above crude graffiti. You can relate to the message. Pausing for a second you salute your fellow chickens living out the little time they have remaining in their lives before they're food. That's what you are. You're food. The world sees you as food. Chew you up, shit you out.

The dead streets feel like you're the only one left in the world. It should be a relief.

No one to see your shame. No one to see you humiliate yourself at the altar of your wife.

But that isn't what it feels like. It feels like there is nowhere to go and nowhere to return to. You're acting on autopilot. One foot following another. Are feet supposed to know where to go?

There's something about the two-faced razorblade of a personality that New York balances on. The brick buildings. The ugly modest storefronts—half of them with Polish names seem like they should be something separate from the glitz and glam of Manhattan. The terrible pretension of the island sucking off the blue collar eagerness; American belief in some kind of meritocracy; hard work wins the day. What a load of shit. The fucking vampires. And Penelope wants to be one of them. You always knew it. It was what attracted you to her at the same time it repulsed you. Made you sick to think of how basic she was. Standard issue.

You thought you could live a normal life through her. But instead of fixing you everything spiraled out of your control.

You're at Manhattan Avenue. Take a right turn.

Malewiski, Malewiski, & Boccio, LLP a law firm's sign announces. Penelope's years in law school put an additional strain on your already broken relationship. She was becoming more professional, you were stuck in neutral.

Your eyes flicker over ragged stores like Max Sportswear and Just Men—the S in "Just Men" was a goofy lighting bolt. There is a modest lo-fi quality to this neighborhood. It feels hidden away from the evil Mordor of skyscrapers and fashion avenues on the other side of the river. The "greatest city in the world" using it as food for its rapacious gullet. Insatiable, it consumes the world to feed its narcissism. Food like you are food.

Walking walking walking down the miserable street lit dirty yellow by the light of closed shops.

Another Polish bakery, another Polish restaurant and you're at another node along your trip. You're relieved to recognize the intersection you were waiting for and make a right at the Dunkin' Donuts across the street from the 99 cent store. The smell of donuts baking smells delicious. Penelope wouldn't eat those now. She was nicer when she was fat.

Your motivation must be coming from the black box because there's nothing you can think of that would justify another step.

Now you're on Bedford. That's your target. The Bedford stop on the L train.

Your stomach turns at the barest wisp of a thought of Bedford Avenue, the Mecca of hipster nation. It fills your head with images of adult children crammed together like cockroaches. Crawling over each other to get into this or that thrift store record store artisanal grocery hand made single use butt plugs. You want to set them all on fire.

But that's crap and you know it. You'd sooner set yourself on fire than hurt anyone. Still, it does feel like a reprieve to hate someone else besides yourself, even if only for a moment.

It's while you're walking through the intersection of Lorimer, Bedford, and Berry that you notice the first person you've seen since you left Penelope's apartment. They're standing there at the tip of one of the intersection's 5 points. They look broken down, disheveled. A homeless? Dirty oversized army surplus jacket, poorly fitting pants, dirty sneakers. Just standing there.

The point of the intersection opens to the tip of a greenspace. It looks like a park surrounded by a low fence. Looking past the homeless man you see a green rectangular plaque secured to the fence. The yellow letters announce its name above the green leaf symbol of the NYC parks and recs department.

You're walking past McCarren Park.

Penelope told you a story she'd heard of people fucking in McCarren after a long night of drinking.

The thought comes to you that the story was not something she'd heard. No. She was relating her own experience through the conceit of a third party.

This realization comes with the associated narrowing of vision, the sound of static, and sense of a hundred thousand needles pricking your skin.

***

When you return to self awareness you find yourself at a cut-through leading west. You realize that you stopped breathing. Your fugue has brought you about a thousand feet down Bedford to a driveway exiting onto the street. A decision has been made and you turn right, veering off the hated Avenue and towards the East River. You walk along the path dividing a large building to the north from some tennis courts to the south that are part of the larger park complex.

A sense of calm follows your change of direction. The calm flows in the way feeling returns to a limb that has fallen asleep. There is a certainty which takes hold of you and carries you along.

The environment seems to change along with your mood, from the lush green of a city park to the rat-maze earnestness of 14th Street's warehouses. They lead you straight to the Manhattan skyline which looms in the distance. The empty desolation of 3 a.m. is alienation amplified by the blank brick buttressing the street. There is nothing to distract you from your destination. The blank walls speak to you, "get the fuck outta here already." They don't care about you.

The closer you get to the shoreline the more the city around you disintegrates into decrepitude—mirroring your mood. You walk past an industrial park containing huge rusting silos and an abandoned green building covered in peeling paint and smashed windows. A self-portrait.

The road past the decaying compound ends at a yellow diamond sign with the word END. It stands in the middle of the road as if guarding the pathetic cyclone fence behind it. The fence divides the end of the street from the East River. It is an old ruined fence which sags longingly towards the unremarkable public housing buildings that wall in Manhattan as if it were Troy.

You stand there next to the sign. "End." You find it hard to imagine what tomorrow looks like.

You put your eggs into her basket and she made an omelette out of you. You sold, gave away, or trashed all your belongings, leaving the apartment you shared together and flying to the east coast in the hopes she would take you back. Doesn't seem to have worked out as you'd hoped.

But, then again, this is what you deserved. You feel like dirt. Worse than dirt. Dirt at least has value. Plants grow from dirt. People make bricks from dirt. You haven't made a single thing that still stands.

It would be better for everyone if you just climb this broken fence and use it like a springboard.

That would be good. You wouldn't have to explain to anyone that your wife is fucking Brooklyn or about how you crawled back through Greenpoint to your mom's house in the middle of the night because you had nowhere else to go.

"Spare some change?"

The gravelly low voice startles you.

So focused on climbing up and over—your sudden lurch of surprise is all the failing fence needs to come loose from the broken earth holding it in place. It sags further towards the river and you find yourself angled on top of it as though relaxing in a hammock. The shame urging you to climb up the fence is cooled by the black water beneath you. Fear rises to your awareness.

Wide-eyed, you look back over your shoulder to the source of the voice. Disheveled and dirty, face worn by exposure, a man stands a few feet behind you.

"Do you mind? I'm kind of in the middle of something right now."

He shrugs. "I mean...you're not going to need it, right?"

You tap your forehead to the rusting metal of the chainlink and close your eyes. After a short pause you slowly crawl in reverse off the fence.

With your feet on solid ground you notice how nice it feels to have your heels support your skull.

You shove your hand into your pocket and pull everything out of it. Your fist contains bills, a napkin, and a stick of gum. The man glances down at it as you thrust it at him.

"Here, take it. Take all of it. I don't care. I don't need it."

"But, then how would you pay for your bus ticket home?" He speaks through wind-chapped lips.

Looking up, you're pretty sure you detect the slightest hint of a smile.

"Wait, what? What did you just say?"

"I'm an alien," he responds.

After everything that has happened you didn't think you could feel more disoriented, but you were wrong. Things just got weird. "Look, I'm not having the best day, can you just take my money and leave me alone?" You wiggle your still-outstretched hand.

"I'm just saying: we don't belong here. Don't you feel that?"

His words are like a dagger in your chest. Your hand drops to your side. "I feel like that all the time. All the time."

"Right. Well, we aliens can't just let each other suffer when we're going through a hard time."

"How do you know I'm having a hard time?"

He points at the fence, "What was that? Sight-seeing?"

You look down at your shoes. "Oh, yeah. Yeah, it's been a bad day." You pause for a moment to think about it. "I lost everything today."

"Everything?" The alien looks around and raises his arms to indicate The Everything appears to be less lost than you insist.

"She doesn't love me anymore." You look up at him, meeting his eyes.

"And she was everything?" A faint odor of copper mixed with sweetgrass smells like it is coming from the man.

"I made myself the person she wanted me to be so that she would take me back."

"Who did she want you to be?"

"Gone. She wanted me gone." You choke down a sob. "Wait, why are you talking to me about this shit? I don't know you. Why am I talking to you?"

"Little brother, I'm going to tell you something I'm not supposed to tell you. Something that could really screw things up." He leans in towards you and you recoil. "The reason I'm talking to you is because I am you."

"Aw, come on, man. A second ago you were an alien." You act annoyed, but you're relieved that the absurdity of this lunatic distracts you from thinking about Penelope.

"Listen, I'm from the future. I'm here to keep us from doing something stupid."

You look at the fence and the river beyond it.

"No. That's not what I mean." He kicks at the dirt with his worn sneaker, then looks up at you, "There is nothing more dangerous to your future right now than thinking that woman's affection has anything to do with your well being. It has nothing to do with you." He grabs your shoulders and focuses on you with a sincere intention, "Your life depends on this."

You pull away from him, crossing your arms. "No. I fucked up. I need to make it right."

"You didn't fuck up, kid. We made mistakes just like every other human being ever born makes mistakes."

"So it was fine? For me to be an asshole?"

"You so sure you're an asshole? Our minds are a black box, kid. We don't know why we do what we do."

You start to protest, but he interrupts you.

"All that screwing around you did was because you thought it was what you wanted. Would you have done it if you thought it would bring you here?"

You hang your head. As loathsome as you feel right now, you know that you'd never wish this feeling on yourself.

"You've been acting out. On auto-pilot. Your whole life. To distract yourself."

"Distract myself from what?"

"From being ok."

"Ok?"

"You're ok."

You bristle and raise your voice, "I'm not ok! I'm fucked up! I'm a fucking cuckold. My wife is probably fucking some hipster right now." You're shouting now. "I dropped everything to follow her here. I told her I loved her. I wanted her. I went out of my way to help her out. She made a fool of me." You throw your hands down and turn away from the man. "And I deserved it! I deserved all of it."

"You're down on yourself. I hear you." He puts his hand gently on your back. "Most of the time it doesn't work the way we wanted. Most of the time what we want isn't what we need. Being a person is messy. It's fucked up. And that's ok. It's not because it's moral or ethical, but because that is what humans do. We fuck shit up and then we pick up the pieces and make the best of it. It's ok. You're ok. You're not a sociopath trying to hurt people because you don't have a heart. That's not you. You're just dealing with your own hurt and your own pain."

You're not quite sure what to do. What this stranger is saying, it doesn't feel right, but it makes sense. And it feels better than walking through Greenpoint. It feels better than climbing the fence.

You turn back to the man. "It's ok? What I did to her all those years?" Your breathing is starting to slow.

"What's ok is right now. Right now, you get to make different choices. That's ok. And speaking of choices, Penelope's her own person and she chose to be with you despite all of it."

"'Til she didn't."

"Sure, she changed her mind. But before she changed her mind she made a choice to be with you. Adults are responsible for their choices. If you aren't making your own choices you're just out of control. You're just a machine, a computer running its program. Is that you? Are you a replicant?"

Replicant? You recognize the word as a reference to the movie Blade Runner.

Your father took you and your brother to see Blade Runner when you were 13. He would take you to see movies that were inappropriate for kids. At 13 you liked the movie because it reminded you of the way you felt every day—dark and miserable.

"No, I'm not a replicant. But, hey, even Roy Batty showed humanity at the end of the movie; so maybe there's hope for me, too, right?"

"The character of Batty showed that none of us are beyond saving. He showed us that even a hunted outcast, someone with no future to look forward to, can still offer compassion to someone who hated him. Harrison Ford hunted Batty and his family the entire movie. During the finale when he's about to lose his grip and fall to his death, Batty saves him. As Batty sits there dying right after that moment he insists that his personal experience was valuable." The man pauses and puts his hand on your shoulder while looking into your eyes. "So, I'm going to ask you again, are you a replicant? Is your experience valuable, even though you were just determined to erase that value permanently?"

You notice your mouth is open before responding.

"Yeah," You say. "I don't know. When I first watched the movie, I thought that Deckard was the hero, but every time I watched it afterwards I had more of a feeling that it was the replicants who were the heroes. They were the ones who were just trying to survive in a world that made them to be servants and to die young."

He takes his hand from your shoulder and stands there in front of you—arms akimbo, "So, you going to answer my question?"

"I don't know if I am a replicant or not. I just know that my experience matters. That I matter." You pause and look up. "That's what you want me to say, right?"

"It'll do for now." The old man grins a yellow crooked smile.

What did you think you were doing coming here to the edge of the river? Why did it take this homeless lunatic to get you to realize you were out of your mind? Things seem shitty right now, sure, but he's right. You do matter. There's more to you than your relationship with your ex-wife. And it is ok to make mistakes. Roy Batty was the hero even though he seemed like the bad guy. You start to feel like maybe there is something to look forward to: learning from this moment and growing.

Your breath comes a little easier.

That is when a chime comes from your right pocket.

It's a text sound. You just received a text.

Your shaking hand reaches for your phone and pulls it out.

You look down at the message from Penelope you hold in your hand. "I'm really worried about you. Please, come home," it says.

You slowly look up to find the man staring right into your eyes.

"Harlow" by Paradox M. Pollack

Proof Through the Night

by Paradox M. Pollack

FOR COLETTE AND ANIKA.

"In sequent toil, all forwards do contend."
- William Shakespeare, Sonnet #60

HOMEWARD

Winter Solstice, 2035, 4:37 p.m.

Dylan spoke into the helmet on his lap, "Time is a spectrum of momentums, with many beginnings and no end."

He looked up to make sure he was alone, not wanting to seem like a madman on the train or an actor rehearsing the Yorick scene from Hamlet.

"Harlow, time isn't numbers on a clock circling a single point. It moves in all directions from as many sources as there are points in space. Time is the composition of all of the universe as it opens like a flower or a river of doors. Time's movement is both step by step and all at once, repeating, yet never the same."

He made this future library of reflections for his daughter as he had every day for as long as he could remember. The glow of the setting sun was warm on his face as he continued,

"My dear, you will be here long beyond me; although I am telling you this, you will still have to experience it on your own, my sparrow."

Dylan was nodding off at the front of the train on the coldest day of the year. Tree limbs bare of leaves sped past the windows. Eighteen months of never-ending attention with his factory foreman job and all its responsibilities, and here he was, recording poetry for his child. That seemed proper. A proper way to end the world.

His long fingers rested on his sleek tarnished-patina green and bronze Helm, balanced nearly weightless on his lap. It seemed an appropriate irony that something so new was made to look like a bronze sculpture from ancient times. He leaned toward it to record. "Our bodies are chronometers that count by heartbeats and breaths. We reconstruct the past and imagine the future. But, to be honest, there is no need to understand time except for our togetherness with each other and nature." He smiled to himself, understanding the strange contradiction of Harlow listening to this in a distant future,"Some day, I'll tell you what I know about eternity."

Dylan caught his reflection in the window, and thought he was looking at his father, who, like him, had been thin and pale. The long hours in the depth of the factory hadn't helped his complexion. Harlow always made a big deal about his face being "spikey" from the beard stubble frequently on his face. He took five minutes to consider his daughter's delicate cheek as he kissed her goodnight once every third week. At least he remembered to shave some of the time.

Dylan's pale green eyes tracked the 3rd story windows and cathedral spires as they raced past. Since childhood, he always sat in the Elevated train's first car and stared at the old factories, churches,and two story homes stretching to the horizon. Over the last weeks, he had watched and marveled as the many railguns, coilguns, and missile batteries started to freckle the rooftops of his youth, all in preparation for this most important night.

He was exhausted as the train car rocked back and forth; his memories merged with the familiar rattle and squeal of the metal and steel, and as his eyelids drooped gazing at the Ben Franklin Bridge he was lulled into sleep.

He dreamt of the hospital during his daughter's birth as he slept. Staring down the long, fluorescent-lit corridors, he realized he couldn't move. The hospital walls shook, and the lights went out. He was lifted like a statue and pressed into a thick, sticky substance. The lights flickered back on while faceless hyena men {clothed in trash bags with raised tattoos and scars like 3-D maps of a mountainous landscape) painted him into the hospital's walls with black tar and honeycomb. Frozen in sleep paralysis, fully conscious but unable to move, he could hear his wife's wailing down the hall. He pressed with all his strength but couldn't get to her.

The brakes screeched. Thundering, the train slowed to a stop. The doors hissed open as Dylan shook himself awake, leaped onto the platform, and into the frigid air. The cold snapped him to attention as the train doors closed behind him.

It embraced his head as a second skull as he put on his Helm. The contained environment of his helmet's noise reduction and atmosphere-regulating functions gave him the feeling of weightless suspension as he stepped across the elevated platform. With his hands in his long, wool coat pockets, he careened down some age-smoothed stairs, his pencil-thin legs scissoring swiftly.

The entire station had been fashioned from the remnants of a 200-year-old fortress. Directional arrows and QR codes patterned the walls in the official font of the New Order. His visor registered the QR code with a familiar hum revealing his current position in the Verses Grid. Maps adjusted, and his Stream came online, updating all his connections and forums. As they poured onto his visor's inner screen, he swiftly exited his media with an extended blink, choosing to remain free from all of the world's opinions.

He looked over the platform balcony and noticed the official hieroglyphics painted in precisely-edged fonts on all of the missile silos on the neighboring rooftops. Only Commanders with proper access would be able to use them. In the distance, he could see a few silhouettes of Technicians close to the batteries as if making sure of their capacities in preparation for the night ahead.

As the rattle-rumble of his train receded into the distance, its echoes ricocheted along the concrete sidewalks and glass display windows. Dylan stretched his neck to see the tracks' smooth steel and riveted pinewood from below as he turned a corner and passed through the turnstiles.

He stopped to look at a metal plaque by the entrance to the station. It read, "Frankford Terminal," built on the original King's Highway, was once a Native American footpath. Thomas Jefferson and Alexander Hamilton walked this road when..."

He started to record, and a tiny red dot flashed in the upper corner of his visor." Frankford Terminal is hard-earned liberty. I've been coming here since I was a child. It was rebuilt and rebuilt, and I never questioned the construction; each time, it looked more modern but never lost its fortress feeling. It had been carved from the vestiges of brick and mortar battlements, complete with murder holes."

The commercial signs above the businesses were replaced in a single week almost two years ago by arrows, simple instructions, and crypto scripts. At the beginning of this strict era, shepherding directions and broadcast instructions defined our behavior. Then, the quick and rigid system slowly became more familiar and automatic.

The arrows indicated a unified society with a singular focus to replace the every-person-for-themselves that had made America what it was since the Declaration of Independence and became the canvas for irreverent beautification. Everywhere along the walls, the access QR code ciphers became the canvas for a collaboration of hundreds of artistic styles. The symbols and directions were left exposed but painted on all sides with mastery by Philadelphia's graffiti artists.

Art had placed a lattice of beauty around the necessary. New murals had appeared daily, beautifying the hard official fonts and revealing them as emergent visions of possibility. The universe forced the hand of society from Independence to Interdependence.

This new society had managed nineteen-hour days for 18 months to complete the missions defined by the orders of society. In preparation for

Alexander, GENIX had created a class of Designers whose job was to organize society around this singular purpose. With their help, the world miraculously came around the bend at the brink of total social chaos. As a result, humanity made a monumental global victory and set a new standard of togetherness.

Recalling all of this, he did his best to say it as simply as possible, "What is made must be maintained. What doesn't resurrect itself, what doesn't reshape its skin, ends up on the Earth's compost heap."

Through a wide stone gateway, Dylan stumbled dizzily onto the empty street. The graffiti continued along the walls and out into the street. The steel grid of the elevated tracks with its old green paint-splattered and webbed with mosaics of shocking colors of symbols, signatures, and cartoon characters. Further from the stairs, the street's yellow dividing lines sank into the distance with white streaks of rock salt across the black asphalt, where the recently melted snow had lost the chemistry war.

He continued to record as he walked onto the empty street. "Invent to destroy. Build to overcome. Once we complete our campaigns, what do we do with the weapons we forged?"

Under the clear skies and descending sun, a knife of cold air cut under Dylan's collar. He tightened the scarf around his neck.

Shadowed by the Elevated train tracks, all of these repurposed stores were eerily silent. Yet, every day for two years and until two days ago, these streets waltzed with purpose. Before dawn, as Dylan made his way to the factory, trucks were unloaded by the local Essentials, and the cadence of humble diligence was still echoing the narrow streets when he returned home long after dark. Everyone's timing had been choreographed by GENIX, but now nothing moved but the cold wind. He drew his long wool jacket tight and smiled with a warrior's determined resolve.

"Time will swallow everything eventually. Time digests the useful and expels the remainder," He recorded into his Helm. It had become a habit, almost an obsession, to record his thoughts for his daughter, Harlow. He reviewed and organized the recordings on the late nights if he didn't pass out. These recordings would be his family legacy if humanity survived the night.

A ringtone voice from a Japanese anime hovered in the closed environment of his Helm, "I'm dreaming, I'm dreaming." It announced that his daughter was calling. A double-blink command produced the audio illusion that she was beside him on the street.

"Daddy?"

He could see her in the lower-left corner of his Helm's visor, in visual contact, yet still able to navigate his walk home.

"Yes, m'dear?"

"Why do we have to eat?"

He smiled to himself. "Well, I told you, 'Low, this is how life happens." Then, his voice shifted to a lively tone, "We eat and digest, then poop, and we are hungry again. Right?" He paused for effect.

"Wake up, go about our day, then we get tired and sleep. It's like a circle. You start drawing it and then make your way back to the beginning. Everything in nature operates in cycles, and people are a part of nature."

She looked up and made a sour face; her dark green eyes flared, "I know, Dad!" Then she returned her focus to the dutiful task of drawing rough blueprint designs with crayons, pastels, gouache, watercolors, and ink pens scattered across the surface of her drawing table.

"Still designing Rudolf?" he asked, his breath pressured by his quick pace.

"Of course! Storytelling androids aren't going to fabricate themselves. At least not yet, anyway." Her snarky smile vanished. "Daddy?"

"Yes, dear?"

"Why do we have to die?"

His steady gait slowed. The Parenting Guild Forum alerts warned that this line of inquiry would become more common as Alexander approached.

What should children feel when adults don't know how the world will change or if we will live to see the next day?

His speech became more deliberate and firm, "We will talk about that when I get home; why don't you tell me what you learned today."

She took a moment to concede her query. "Ok."

As she spoke, she occasionally scribbled, looking up to see Dylan's reactions, "So, GENIX made our class walk back through time. We just kept going back and back until there were only forests and trees where we live now, and we kept walking and walking in every direction. It was just a beautiful forest with little streams everywhere and animals. It was so nice to hear the birds chirping and the wind in the trees. We met some nice people. We sat with them, and they told a story about how animals made the world. It was such a cool story. As we listened, our class made animations of turtles and eagles leaping and falling from the sky to the ground while the people... What was their name, Rudolph?"

"The Lenni-Lenape, Ms. Harlow." Rudolph's gentle and generous well, crafted synth voice replied.

"Who?" Dylan asked.

"The nice people. They were called the Lenni-Lenape. That's a great name, right? So I tried to ask the Lenni-Lenape why they don't live here anymore, but GENIX wouldn't let me. I tried to get Rudolph past protocols, but he couldn't. GENIX just repeated that if I wanted to know, I should ask permission from you. So, Dad, what happened to the people who lived in the forest?"

"Progress," Dylan smirked with cynicism.

"Progress? I don't get it."

"Well, pumpkin, we logged the forests to build the city. What do you think happened to the people who lived in the forest?"

"Why did we kill the forest? Why couldn't we just live there with the nice people? They seemed happy."

Dylan's mind composed a dozen responses in the following moments of silence. "It was the best we knew at the time," excused us from all responsibility. He shook his head. Best to just be honest. "We destroyed the forest to make our cities. But we didn't destroy them all, 'Low. Some were preserved. Fairmount Park is the biggest in the country. Hopefully, tomorrow," his voice cracked on the word, "I can take you out there." He hoped she hadn't noticed the fear bottled up in his voice.

"Do the nice people still live there?"

"No, honey, they've been gone long ago. We might see some deer or a raccoon, though."

"Dad?"

"Yes, Low?"

"Today, I was asking Rudolph about Civil War Two. He showed me some information and old pictures from the First Civil War. Why Dad? Why do we fight each other like that?"

"People do many things without thinking about what it means in the long run, kiddo. For instance, if you don't eat, you will get crazy cranky, right? So, just eat the Sim-food, ok? Things will change soon."

She winced. "I'll eat it, but I won't like it."

"How's Rudolph coming along?"

"He's getting better. I just don't have the tools that I need. So I petitioned the Designer's guild."

She sighed," What no one gets is that GENIX can't lead. It can," she held up her fingers to the camera. Finger one, "solicit attention," finger two, "make hierarchies of questions," finger three, "create achievement games. The Designers still don't know what it can do, and GENIX only follows their lead."

"No one knows what it is capable of, honey, but I know you can figure it out."

"Yeah, I will if we survive tonight. But, dad, I wanna understand how we could be so selfish. Why were people mean for all that time, and why did we make things in such a stupid way?"

Silence.

"More questions with no good answers. What is it with this kid?"

Dylan noted his route coordinator and retracted his visor with a touch to the right side of his Helm. The cold air stung his eyes. "I'll be there in thirteen minutes and twenty-three seconds. Finish your lessons, and we'll talk after."

He resisted the urge to bring his visor down again. The Helm's integrated quantum computer was now just a warm hat with a telephone.

"Ok, Dad. See you later."

"Bye Boo, love you."

He took the time to enjoy walking without focusing on anything, his eyes seeing what they viewed naturally, without augment. Every day, he used his Helm to consider every aspect of his factory and its products with microscopic lensing. The data streams linked his progress with millions of others in the coordinated production of the last 2 years.

NEW STREAM

The old wooden porch was speckled with chipped paint, which Dylan had neglected. His numb hands implored him to go inside, but he found his pockets instead. He sat and reflected on his history, knees stretched wide, elbows on thighs, head resting on hand, a lean Rodin's Thinker.

He took a few breaths and slowed his mind to see the big picture. He was good at this, and he wanted to try and let it all in. He left his eyes open and allowed his breath and the sensations of his body to become one singular experience. He felt a hypnagogic state between being asleep and awake arrive.

Calculating the distance to the horizon, past the patterns of heat and wind, he wondered if this was the last sunset he'd ever see. But, as a responsible citizen, one could only trust that the world and his team had done their best. His work was done. His factory and team had manufactured six hundred thousand tons of vibratory fabric over the last eighteen months, "sound-and-solar-sails" crafted to control gravity. These would guide the Asteroid fragments out of the atmosphere if all went well.

It was up to the Commanders, whose ships were positioned between the moon and the planet. Our one line of defense against the world-killing mass of Alexander. In 2033 the UN created the AAC, a military-adjacent peace-keeping global public service, to enforce international law through The Global Continuance Act. The AAC was focused on one purpose: Eradicating the doomsday curse sent from the stars. For our world to survive, these trained combatants must filet a mountain. They would take it apart with a stone surgery with bombs for a scalpel. Nuclear weapons blast constellation fractures to shatter the Asteroid into measured fragments.

After almost two years, all the exogenous planning, designing, training, and practice of the AAC units moved from rehearsal to the galactic stage. Two hundred and fifteen spaceships coordinated their attack patterns in the magnetosphere at speeds that burn steel to ash on Earth.

The citizens of his neighborhood were miles away; those without "final details" had made their way to the closest location of the global celebration of life called "The Hailing." It was a victory ceremony for the whole world. We had done our best, and now we would see what we were worth. Every family or individual chose a site to watch the greatest show, possibly the last show on Earth.

He released his hands from their meditation pose, noticed the sun turning the sky to redder shades of destiny, and decided to document for Harlow.

"Memory seems to me to be an instrument of necessity. As sense data arrives in the Stream of consciousness, memory puts itself in the way to remind us of previously successful strategies. Is it from our childhood? Is it from the memories of ancestors long past hunting that lives in the fibers of our DNA?"

A few images traced in his mind as he spoke these words. The repetition of the threading loom, the sweat on his team's brows as they circled to assess the day's progress, a cigarette stolen in the back alley with his Helm in his other hand. The movement of the machines stitched the vibratory fabric. The details of a circuit board pattern. He saw his factory in synchronized activity, a dozen freeze-frames of his work as the overseer of the Weavers. Threads and the shuttle moving along perfect A.I.-assisted lines. An empty screen with a blinking cursor and then a flash of himself at Harlow's age, sitting on the same porch.

"Memory is a parallel course along two rivers. The waters are deeper than we can see. Memory commandeers our senses and leaves us like a fish suspended in time, holding our place in a rushing stream, watching the world as a shapeable dream."

His memories came instantly of Francine, shining golden ghosts of his wife shimmering through time from dozens of sunsets like this one.

With their dogs leading the way, they nearly crashed into each other, looking at their phones. Francine's irritation changed as they found each other's eyes.

Within minutes, they laughed at how old their dogs were and how difficult it had become to be isolated for so long. Despite the plague, two people found each other and fell in love. They didn't leave the tree shade until the dogs started whining to go home. The inconsiderate bitches.

From their first parting, he remembered her response, "I guess I'll see you when I see you," he said shyly.

"Only if I see you first."

In the wake of that memory he was drawn back to the cold and the immanence of fear and focused on the sensor array that he used to test his factory product daily. The project assigned to him by the AAC was to harness the power of the sun and transform it into vibration, turning cosmic weather into potential and power.

"Memory is all our precious moments queued up and loaded behind our eyes, waiting to be synched to our destiny."

The three-story row home where they were raised had its own life threaded through generations. His family was typical Irish, held together by time-tested brainwashing, fear of neighborly judgment, and profound ignorance about what it meant to be satisfied.

Emblematic of Philadelphia streets since the ancient city's beginning, the bricks that housed centuries of grit, toil, and sweat were now swarming with pure data. A planetary library, the sum of the ages within their walls, customized to each household's interests and needs. In 2030, humanity was given full access to global information banks; they needed it to survive. After its first meeting in Geneva, the AAC proclaimed, "We will die together, or we have a choice: to live together."

"Record: Everyone creates a password between themselves and the world, separated by airlock waystations. After Alexander, we did our jobs without getting in each other's way. We simply had to get along. As our ancient ancestors who survived the ice age, we understood this without saying it."

PERSONAL POSSESSIONS

Dylan removed his HYDRON from his Helm and gently placed it into the Black Box just inside the door. As he set it into place, it made a magnetic snap. He shut the lid, and a whirring sound accelerated past his hearing range. The lights grew slightly brighter as the Black Box began to charge the sonic black hole in a tiny droplet of water at the center of his eight-sided HYDRON. Dylan remembered his attempts to understand how the superconductive polyhedron shapes, magnetics, velocity, and sound all generated quantum envelopes in water at a subatomic level that altered the fabric of information and power. It was beyond him; even though the animations had made sense, the impossibility of the result still boggled his mind.

Once the HYDRON was in the Black Box, it instantly provided the house with enough data to fill a mountain of mainframes. In addition, the isofrequency surfaces adjacent to the churning void at its center could store enough power to run the electronics in the house for a month.

Power and information beyond our wildest imagination had been swiftly accepted, adopted, and almost forgotten. Yet, this miracle slipped in alongside language, air, and transatlantic cables as one of the invisible elements that sustained the world and kept it alive.

Dylan put his verdigris Helm next to the other three on the shelf. Harlow's sleek Nike Helm shone like sapphires suspended in clouds, and he took an extra moment to wipe the cobwebs from Fran's dust-dulled salmon pink.

Just down the hall, he went to the door of the Medset room where his wife was receiving her treatments. He opened the door and looked in. The entire room had been refitted to the long bed-like treatment table she lay suspended on. He took her in for a moment, noticing her long and coiling hair and her smooth brown skin, and dreamed again the fiction of her sitting up and catching his eyes. In the fantasy, they embraced, and he dipped her deep in a dance while they kissed. He measured her breathing from the door; they were both still as water in a melting ice cube.

With a gesture in the air, he indicated to GENIX. He scanned the readout of Francine's current condition, which was projected at his request at eye level. He checked the readings and approved the Medset's new cycle of adjusted therapies. Her status was the best he had seen for months. She was in the upper ninety-seventh percentile of neurological activity. Looking more closely at the data pictograms, everyone was making a marked recovery. Was it possible to see recovery from katastrophen narcolepsis? There was no report yet of anyone waking from the mental virus. Could it be they all sensed the arrival of Alexander? He allowed himself a particle of hope.

He allowed himself a moment to record as he walked out of the hall and toward the living room. "GENIX, Record," calibrating his new environment to the settings of his Helm," imagination is a seed that will grow no matter what you feed it. For a garden to flourish, you have to prune the weeds. Don't throw them away. Just turn the weeds upside down so their roots are in the air; they feed the soil just fine. We don't want them to steal water and nutrients from the ideas that nourish us."

ONCE A CIRCLE CLOSES, THERE IS NO RETURN

When Dylan was a child, his father, Arthur, had his Father-chair. No one else sat in that chair. It seemed like a tradition from the 1950s; a Bing Crosby Christmas song. Still, Dylan wondered if it was a carryover from time immemorial: The man's place, his throne, no matter how humble, was a part of the framework of the human home. Dylan fell into his Father-chair as the holo-projection field went from fuzz to focus, and the speaker arrays aligned to his position. He sourced through a few of his favorite skins, one where he was a driver in an El Camino, another where he was seated on an Atlantean temple throne. Finally, he chose a lush forest where all media data came skinned with fruits, flowers, and seeds.

Dylan rode a hummingbird in the holographic interface, viewing the multiple Inter-GENIX and Enter-GENIX Streams from above to pick and trigger his chosen Stream.

"Record: Imagination is a map wherein one can travel between any number of coordinates or see the whole map and search for its edges. The horizon breeds dragons."

Dylan began his career fifteen years ago; he knew little about light, sound, heat, and gravity. He hadn't studied science, feeling that it had cheated and created the world as we know it. Yet, after managing his project to completion, he knew everything about the visible spectrum, phononic black holes that produced megawatts of power, and the Infrared and UV index.

"Record: Imagination tells a story to match the universe's functions. From the unconscious mind, formulations of equations are proven undeniably true. For example: Through transformation, an amphibian or butterfly increases its dimension from water to land or land to the sky."

Dylan stared out into space. In his mind, he was standing on the factory floor. Every spinning, weaving, heat-sealing, stitching, and folding machine is quiet and cooling for the first time in eighteen months. He saw the factory one year earlier, full of activity and the roar of the great rolling looms. Then today, "Lights out."

ALEXANDER AND THE ASTEROID SLEEP

Dylan leaned back in his padded reclining massage chair, exhaled, and landed his hummingbird on a tree limb. His muscles were agitated, the side of his face tense. He scanned a spread of current media below from his thin branch, his weight bending it at the fork. The display resembled a hybrid of a flower blossom, a hand of cards spread in four directions, and a compass overlaying a patchwork quilt of maps.

His subscription feeds were organized into categories, each with its customized symbol. His choices were presented as news bubbles, entertainment offers, and participatory games from various Streams. The current status of the Commanders as they approached Alexander was vivid and prominent, superimposed on any of his other choices. In addition, the system constantly updated new trust-and-quality metrics to prioritize whatever task his mind could imagine.

As they approached Alexander, he opted into the Stream of the Commanders with a touch and aligned with their POV. The Asteroid in the games gave way to the real thing: City-sized, of indescribable weight. The density of its relevance made it god-like. Frozen, Dylan struggled to move.

The readouts of top-ranked gamers playing the roles of ship navigators, gunwale battery marksmen, underside bomb deployment, tool, and instrument puppeteers performed all spaceship functions. Each vessel had an arsenal, and each part was operated by a Stream-connected infantry.

The Mesh (a neural signal transmitter) allowed every individual unit to become a part of a global transmission sequence. The pilots had trained beyond their capacity through the interface of options provided by eighteen months of accumulated simulations, AI strategy-adjustment algorithms, and live recommendations from the world's best players. Gamers and Admin forking choices to interpret and give the pilots vital opportunities, mapping five minutes or three seconds into the future. It was an ornately intricate ritual in which nearly every household played a part. Dylan and Harlow had put in consistent gameplay since it began. Yet, now only the top players appointed by the AAC would be broadcasting their updates to the consoles of the Commanders directly.

He ended his link to the Internet, touched his ring finger to his palm, and the IntraNet came online. He leaned back in his Father-chair and entered an access code. Fran's Halo activated and connected her Mesh with Dylan's. He began to share memories, pictures, and video impressions from his life as he drew them from his Drives. They orbited him, slowly moving around him.

This year marked fourteen years since his mother died, twelve since he met Fran, ten since she got pregnant, and eighteen months since the shock of the impending Asteroid took Fran from the waking world. One out of fifty-thousand people got it; the Asteroid simply cut the cord and took them offline.

The Halo connection linked his thoughts to images and videos surrounding him in the XR holographic space. The memories flooded. He and Fran began passionately and then teetered rockily, but Harlow came in like a fresh wind bearing the Spring. One image circled around and became more opaque, filling his whole frame of reference. Fran was pregnant, and his hands' threaded fingers supported the weight. His unborn daughter is in the belly of his wife.

Francine had challenged him, broken his heart, then made him a father and a better man. From the moment of Harlow's birth, any thoughts of getting ahead or making a name for himself just folded into their world. They were all that mattered. Fran and Harlow were the gravity that his life would spend orbiting 'til the end; he held that orbit in the circle his fingers made around his wife's pregnant belly.

Initially, Francine had been just sleeping for long hours, sometimes days, before her diagnosis. Then, six months ago, she simply stopped waking. So finally, they were issued a MedSet. It moved her limbs around, vibrated her organs, gave her injections, and ordered refills; all the caregiver needed was to monitor the feed. Fran received her daily sonic ozone tent treatment and an infusion of psilocybin synthetic with ongoing visualization and musical stim programs.

Medicine was no longer a predatory extraction. Every therapy that showed any success could be given unfettered resources. It was a planetary evolution that left everyone shaking their heads as to why it took so long to provide the care every citizen required. Surrounded by these images of Fran and Harlow, he slipped into a dream.

He stood in a hallway. A hallway stretched as far as he could see until it disappeared into a black tar shadow. Raggedly stitched to the walls was a fine weave of mirrored polymer fabrics. The fragments reflected bright, radiating sound waves that swirled like light bars on the top of a cop car. There, not there. He could see the sound. There, not there. The sound waves echoed the length of the wall's mirrored reflections. The sound was trapped in the mirror, revealing a museum of souls displayed for split seconds.

Inside the kaleidoscope of the wall were the contents of a bee's nest. It had suspended pupae in hexagonal chambers. A deadline dread rushed upon him like the world depended on him. He was a fly in a web of honey, his breath was labored, and his body trembled as Harlow walked from behind him, stepped through the mirrored wall, and climbed into one of the larval chambers. He reached out for her and screamed.

GALLOWS HUMOR

An alert of the Commanders' mission status signaled him awake with a haptic buzz in his Halo. A hovering counter in the room ticked down miles and minutes. He wrinkled his nose, rolled his eyes, and then, still half-asleep, opted-in to one of the top trending "Hailing" headliners.

Cindy Schüld was an emcee of the hundreds of intra-lingual worldwide Hailings, linking the Streams to whichever act or band was ready to "Rock the world at the end of time."

She had her big break ten years earlier, a hit comedy special live from Chernobyl entitled "The bomb would be better."

She was a grim and terrifying figure, gaunt and 6'3", and dressed in a pink, heavily-tailored dress. She could imitate anyone and had shamed past and present political figures with her character assassinations.

She was right in the middle of her signature phrase, "OH MY GOD!"

Everyone screamed with her, and then they laughed.

"Now, you're gonna hate me for this, ahem, but let's be honest; let's be simple like a heart attack, an iron lung, your spouse asleep at the wheel. The entire human enterprise has been a dirty diaper baby dropped off in the middle of the highway," her voice was shrill and melodic, with a thick German accent. "We couldn't care for ourselves without GENIX, so now it will take care of us. In other words, you little brats, we're being ruled by a tin can with a brain the size of the sun.

Tonight's next act on the global stage needs no introduction, but it's my job. Brought together tonight by Trent Reznor and David Grohl, with all the rock and roll survivors of the last 100 years. Let's see if you recognize them... they call themselves "The Gordian Nots!"

PARALLAX ADJUST

"Dad, what's happening on the Tele?"

He instinctively clapped his hands shut, and the Stream closed.

Harlow stood by the wall of the hall that led to her room. Her long curls of hair radiated to the middle of her back, and the tilt of her head told Dylan that she was heavy with her thoughts. As Harlow walked toward him, he noticed her confident stride, reminding him of himself. Her freckles seemed to jump off her coffee-colored skin as she came closer. Her green eyes sparkled as the lights shifted from the hologram radiance to a full spectrum white.

"Hi, my sparrow; I didn't see you there. Come here."

They embraced. Father held daughter for a long time as only a parent can, the continuity of so many times asleep in those same arms. Then, she sat on the floor at the base of the chair. Dylan looked at her face, inquisitive and demanding. Harlow made the open-palmed gesture she'd used since she was four, indicating she wanted to play the "Why? game".

Dylan's eyebrow raised, and after a moment, he nodded. She smiled slightly and began.

"Daddy, you never answered my question: Why do people have to die?"

"Well," Dylan paused, measuring the stakes, "Death is a part of life. They are the same thing. The same as how water can be ice and mist and snow, or even a part of us."

"But, why, though?"

"We're all part of the universe. We're always changing, Harlow. We have to so that we can keep learning how to survive."

"But, if death is a part of life, why do we care so much about surviving?"

After a moment, Dylan responded, "Well, I guess because we are given life as a gift. So we have to tend to it. We have to grow it, the same as a garden."

"Why?"

"Because God," he said wryly, as this was his answer when he could no longer answer her questions. They smiled at each other in an often-shared, familiar moment.

The scheduled alert arose from the wall screen: Harlow's bedtime. She frowned, then jumped up and cartwheeled to the door.

She looked back at Dylan and smiled. Next, as was the resource-preserving protocol, she brushed her teeth and took a sonic shower with a quick rinse of water afterward. Then, finally, she put on her pajamas.

Dylan walked to Francine's room. He was at the door, and quietly, reverently, he approached Francine in her Medset tent. Dylan pulled back the oxygen fabric, which accordioned invisibly into the bed frame, lifted her out, and walked her toward their bedroom. As Harlow caught up with him in the hall, there was a strange and somber atmosphere like a bubble of peace and togetherness. Harlow popped it with a question. "Dad, do you think robots dream?"

"Huh?"

"When they get turned off, do they dream or just stop?"

"I think they probably just stop."

"Mom is different, though, right? She's still on. I can see she's dreaming." The tick in the side of Dylan's face started to rumble.

It felt awkward. This was the moment that Dylan was dreading. He laid Fran's body down on their bed, and as they entered, the feeling of the outside world flickered lights into the room.

He knew it was wrong, but he wanted it to be over. He wanted to see if we would die or not. He wanted Fran to wake up and be there with them; he wanted Harlow to just curl up with them as she had as a child, but he didn't know how to say any of that, so instead, he said, "Let's kiss Mommy goodnight and go to bed."

"Is Mommy why we can't go to the Hailing?"

"Yes, BB."

"Ok, then, I'm not mad. We are here together. That's what Mom would want. Goodnight, Mommy."

"Goodnight," he echoed without thinking.

"Can't we sit up and watch the party on Tele?"

He thought about it for a moment. "Sure, I guess. It's all broadcasting live right now. So whatever you want to watch, I'll probably fall asleep."

"Forget it, then. I changed my mind. I don't want to watch the Tele anyway. Can we stay here and sit with Mom? Is that ok?"

He nodded.

They cautiously got onto the bed, and Harlow curled up with her mother. Dylan removed his shoes and stretched across the covers. Francine was there breathing. They both wanted her to call out one of her famous one-liners. They wanted her to jump up and break the ice. It was a while before either of them spoke. Eventually, Harlow broke the silence.

"How do you write a story?"

"That's a good question. What was the story you

read with Francine today about?"

"Two dogs and a cat trying to get home. It made me cry. It had a good ending, though. The whole time we read, I imagined Mom trying to get home to us."

After a pause, he said, "To answer your question, I think, to write a story, you have to sit with the characters for a little while. You think about them and make them part of your everyday life. Then you can start a sentence."

"I want to write a story about Mommy. I don't like to look at her when she sleeps. I feel she's lost in there, and when she used to wake up, she was the same Mom, but now she's been gone so long... I know she's trying to get home."

The tic around Dylan's eye went off, and his chest hurt from the tobacco smoke during breaks.

Then Harlow asked, "Can we just tell a story about Mom?"

NEVER ENDINGS

"Ok," he said.

They shifted on the bed. Francine was in the middle, her passive presence like a cairn enshrined to hold a place for her life. It was just wide enough for the three of them. Father and daughter got close and snuggled into her.

Francine in the long pink nightgown they picked out from the store. It felt soft and smooth to Harlow. Francine's breathing alternated between steady and halting. Was it different than usual?

Dylan began, "Once upon a time..."

Harlow interrupted, "Do we have to start with that? What does that even mean?"

Just as quick, "It means all stories must begin with a place and a time. Can I start now?"

"Yes."

"Once upon a time, there were three robots: Rudolf,"

"That's my robot!"

"Yes, BB, there were two others as well. Zero-range, and Catanius. They were each made of different metals. Rudolf was made of gold, and he thought of things that connected the world: Roads, bridges, and--."

"Circuits."

"Yes, circuits. The second robot, 0-range, was made of iron. 0-range thought of all the weapons and made all the tools that shape the Earth and stone, that cut wood and cook food."

"And what does the third one do?"

"Catanius was made of copper, and it made instruments that measure, such as screens and lenses that could read the sky and listen to the universe. So Catanius was an instrument that could tune itself and talk to the universe."

"One night, Rudolf looked at the wide ocean of stars and asked, 'What makes light?'

Rudolf could see a pattern in the constellations and opened his eyes until he could see the whole sky at once, the vast bowl of the atmosphere's circumference."

"You call it a bowl because it's curved, right?"

"Yes, pumpkin. So Rudolf was looking out at the stars."

"You mean up at the stars."

"No, my sparrow, there is no up, only out and in."

Her head tilted to let that thought in at an angle. "Oh, right. I get it. OUT to the stars and IN to the center of the Earth." She focused on him again as he resumed.

"Yup. So, Rudolf looked out to the stars, and with a gust of wind, 0-range flew in with her fission fuel wings, and said--."

Francine let out an audible sigh. Dylan paused his story, and he and Harlow looked at Fran. She pivoted, her lips twitching. Something was happening there, inside her. Dylan and Harlow both felt it.

"Dad, can we be in the story too? I want to be right there with her."

"Yes, 'Low." Dylan directed his attention out the window. As quiet as their room was, The Great Work was happening outside. Beyond his window surged a field of swirling red and white rays. Occasionally a light passed through the window.

He could barely see the cityscape with so many pinpoints of drone and helicopter lights in the air.

The sun's twilight was spreading its final shimmer, the farthest gamma midnight at the indigo skyline. Dylan and Harlow both focused on the sky's prismatic milk of motion from the bed. They were excited and terrified, not wanting to evaluate Francine's state, not wanting to be disappointed again. Instead, they stared together into the expectant future of the sky where, with certainty, Alexander would arrive.

He spoke out loud:

"Somewhere between imagination and memory is the waking world. In the ocean, currents swell between the waves. When the cadence between wave and current aligns, there is a tide."

Harlow tilted her head to let in this idea, "What's that from, Daddy?"

"I've been thinking all day and recording little messages for you about memory and imagination, and now here we are, all of our memories and possibilities in the balance."

The room was quiet; they could hear Fran's breath steady and slow. Then, finally, Harlow asked in a gentle voice that matched the silence, "How is this a story about Mommy?"

Dylan trailed off as he realized he had no idea where this story was going.

Sensing this, Harlow said, "Dad, I can tell this better."

"Ok, boo, you go."

"This story is about Mom. She has been deep in the underground talking with Earth, and Earth gave her a gift. The Earth gave Mom this gift and told her to return to the world. Mom is dressed in flowers and soft vines tied together; she looks like a queen and is quiet, like when she used to sit alone and think. She has been walking for a long, long time. She is walking through a long corridor and looking for the door. Rudolf opens the door for Mom. The hallway isn't there anymore. It's just a big door, and everyone on Earth, and all the plants and the animals, are there. They enter a big room for everyone, but the robots can't come in. The Guardian Lions say that they aren't allowed. Mom walks inside, and you go in with her, but I'm out there with Rudolph and 0 and Catanius. Everything is in this room: Aliens, the gods from all history... I'm outside, trying to help our robots to make a new robot that would be allowed in. While the gathering makes all this noise and everybody takes their seats, our three robots make a platinum robot that looks just like a person, thinks like a person, and can dream. A one-of-a-kind cyborg guide that we haven't made yet. The cyborg walks in, and there are ALL the animals. I see you two, you and Mom, in the front row, and I sit with you."

There was a sound that they hadn't ever heard from the MedSet, like a ringing bell suspended in honey. Francine twitched between them. They paused, assessing her, frozen in hope. Francine's breath returned to a sleep rhythm. They both relaxed and took an audible breath together, their expectations pouring out.

Dylan said, "Let me take it from here."

They had done this since she was a tiny baby, a call-and-response story tag that started in the coos and gurgles of her first year.

Dylan picked up where Harlow left off, "The room is full of people deciding something historic. Then, as the platinum android walks down the hall past the mammals, buffaloes, monkeys, bears, and mice, they nod at the android. The turtles, lizards, dragons, geckos, and reptiles are spread out on their own little benches. They nod to the android, too. Strange people made of gas and color acknowledge the android. The plant elementals shake their branches and leaves at the android. In another section, all monsters, a centaur, pegasus, a snaketopus, and a jackalope are together."

"What's a snaketopus?" Harlow looked over at him with an eyebrow raised.

He stretched out his fingers, mocking up the octopus body with his palms and thumbs, undulating his tentacle fingers while hissing through a pucker face. Harlow was amused and impatiently completed his sentence, "The monsters nod to the android. Yup, Just as the platinum android gets near the front--." Dylan continued

"What's his name?" she interrupts.

"How do you know it's a he?"

She thinks with the physicality she learned from cartoons. "I don't think the platinum android is a girl or a boy. Can we just call robots' per,' short for 'person'?"

He smiled. "Ok, that's good. So what's per's name? It's a new kind of being. It should be something good."

"You just said it, Dad, a new,' spelled A-N-U."

"Ok. So, ANU gets up to the front near us. Just as he gets there, a massive door opens at the front of the room, behind the Judge's podium. The door is made of all the metals, and a great light pours into the room, and a very old man with purple robes that shimmer like the sun on a river comes out."

"Is it God?"

Dylan paused, "Sure. "

Harlow took over the story, "So, if I have this right, and this is God, what is he doing? Is he deciding who owns the Earth? Is this a court case with God on his judgment seat for who owns the Earth?"

"Sure," Dylan said as he watched his daughter make sense of the world's end.

After a pause, Dylan's eyes closed involuntarily. Harlow took his silence as permission to continue, and she said, "Mommy-Earth stood up and looked around at all the people. Standing to the side was a man in dark robes. His skin was pale white, but there was a rainbow in the shadows of his face. Momma Earth knew he was the story keeper. She made a challenge to the story keeper. Time froze, and the story keeper invited Mom to his house. She went to the story keeper's house, saying, 'I am the Earth. If you give people a good dream, I won't make earthquakes, droughts, floods, or fires that choke the air. Give them a good dream, and I won't make a virus that makes them all go underground.'

"The life-keeper refused, saying, 'Humans are only a temporary thing, as all things are temporary.' As he said this, his sister, the death-maker, popped out of nowhere. So the life-keeper proposed that instead, they look at what happened to people and find the sick part that always makes us fight. He said they should look for what could make us better. Dad, remember you told me about that guy who stole fire from the Gods?"

"Prometheus."

"Yeah, and after he took it, humans got to do whatever they wanted, and then Zeus made the box with the girl?"

"Pandora. Yeah, 'Low, you remember."

"Of course, I remember, I remember everything. Zeus was jealous. He was angry that we got to do whatever we wanted, but he figured out how to put us in Earth prison, and we were angry, too, so we hurt the Earth." She paused and tilted her head. "So now, we must see if people can care for themselves without them."

He tilted his head to try and read her expression. "Without whom?"

Her eyes were as focused as a sniper's. "Without the gods."

WITHOUT THE GODS

Dylan recoiled in response as the soft shock emanated from Harlow's hands. An electric impulse rippled and traversed the bed. Francine gasped, and as her eyes opened, the sky flashed outside their window as bright as noon for a split second, and they were all blinded. Francine's first moment awake was spent blindly groping for her beloved husband and child. They reached instinctively for each other at the center of the bed. Twenty-five seconds later, that seemed a world's worth of wishes come true; they held each other. Unable to say a word that might relay the awe of Francine's return, they were completely silent until a thundering whump rattled the house. The windows shattered, and they could hear the glass of a thousand panes from the neighborhood as the cold air rushed in. Then, as their vision reasserted itself, a massive pink and violet blossom appeared above the sky, carrying the concussive rage of outer space into our atmosphere.

The force of the wave blasted the three of them from the bed, disconnecting Fran from her Medset. They remained huddled together on the floor as shadows flashed on the wall. The sky rippled into light and activity. A distortion in the visual field made it hard to see what happened across the long lens of the atmosphere. The atmosphere lens bent in waves of blue and white, echoing for a moment the rhythm of clouds on a sunny day. Then, long streaks of missiles fired from their rooftops, thousands of thread- traces in the night sky.

They turned together to look through the glassless window into a new sky erupting in blooms of every color. It was impossible to see the difference between the explosions above the atmosphere, and the ones below, a mirrored horizon to eternity.

The Jazz

by Matt Bitonti

Oswald's hands started to tingle. He winced as if his fingertips were over an open flame. The endless cold that froze his extremities backed off, beginning with the blisters at the edge of his fingertips. Waking invariably began with this maelstrom of sensation he called 'the jazz.'

Others had different names for it: the tingle, the pep, the zapp, the stab, the juice. Whatever the name, they woke him up and restored his humanity once a year, just to keep him alive. It was the bare minimum.

Of course, he'd been through it enough to know what to expect. It went downhill fast, as post-tingle, he'd sweat, shiver, cough, and choke just to breathe. His muscles ached so badly he wished he didn't have arms or legs. The catch was, right as he felt like a complete person again, they put him back on ice, which was, quite frankly, how Oswald preferred to exist.

But that was a problem for after the jazz, a sensation so unique, so genuine, he dreamt about it.

The jazz felt like the sun rising over the hillside on a bitter March morning, thawing the frozen land that looked dead.

Knowing the real itch from the fake could be tricky. Oswald tried to remember. The authentic jazz started from the outside and worked inward. Everything else went the other way. Without warning, the feeling retreated, and Oswald's senses came alive.

opposite: "The Jazz" by Simon Adams

***

He crouched among the verdant, thick jungles of a terraformed planet. The gravity too heavy for Mars, it could have been Venus or even Earth itself. He was shooting, without armor, union-busting one of the crews that constantly wanted more. His rifle pushed recoil into his sore right shoulder, and he flinched as bombs rocked the landscape.

The stifling jungle air coated his brow, the sweat drowning his aim. But he could see his targets, shadowy snipers up in the treetops. They prepared for him; the rebels had the steam turned up full blast. He crawled through the murky bog, darting between the grasses and the reeds. He held his breath among the fetid blackwater and peered his silenced rifle upward. Oswald squeezed twice. He heard two airy pops, followed by two splashes into the swamp.

Oswald's neck hair stood, so he turned and brought his aim around. Mid turn, he encountered an insane noise, a scream or laughing shriek. He found two bearded monkeys caught in an embrace and another, smaller specimen, clinging white-knuckled to the trunk of a tree. Oswald held his fire, even though they and the cream-dappled exotic bird all turned to look. Deep into his soul, the creatures stared.

A deep shiver and he felt the jazz again—it was another dream. The timing wasn't predictable to him on a conscious level as he had no conscious level. Nevertheless, like a man waking one minute before his alarm clock, Oswald felt it coming somehow.

The best practices said that humans could only dream, stock-still, for exactly three-hundred and sixty-four Earth days before risking damage. What was a year? A minute, an hour, twenty-four hours in a day had no relevance on a space station this far out, where the sun had the brightness of a flashlight pointed down a dark hallway. Nonetheless, his life measured in Earth days and Earth years, or that's what they told him when it was time for him to wake.

Humanity had long since mastered the wide-ranging skills needed for suspended animation. First, the gene splicing, introducing the cold-blooded mechanisms of the cold-blooded. While on ice, Oswald's blood glowed a metallic green, a bioluminescent nod to the wood frogs that provided much of the code. The glow was temporary, but it had been green so long,

Oswald worried his glacier-chilled blood forgot how to be red. He had small gills implanted in his nostrils, allowing a passive replacement for breathing. Obviously, none of it was possible without the nano-bots, ever circulating and repairing damaged cells. But the final step, vitrification, proved to be the most challenging and had required the most sacrifice of human test subjects. Given time and the invention of organic friendly anti-freeze, the process of cooling his squishy liquid bag-cells below the temperature of what should be solid ice proved routine.

For those travelers en-route to the outer planets (and beyond), the "long nap" was a boon. Waking before they reached their destination was unnecessary. For journeys of a few weeks or even a few months, stasis proved a stable and even pleasant way to travel the stars.

But even to the point which humanity had perfected it, long-term suspended animation, or X-Stasis, had limits. And for long haulers, prisoners, and those with massive debt outstanding (like Oswald), the limit was an ever-pressing concern. Officially, all humans had to breathe natural air, eat a meal, and generally thaw out at least one day out of every Earth calendar year or risk permanent brain curdle. But like the expiration date on freeze-dried protein, Oswald considered the guidelines more like suggestions.

* * *

Again the jazz receded, and Oswald attacked. This time he was flying and shooting among the void. The debris from his targets left trails in the vacuum. A quick status check told him he was outside the Ganymede colony, chasing some poor souls down into a rock cavern. Water-miners on strike for a living wage, but their suits were garbage, and their weapons a joke. Oswald took what the battle offered. Brown slate plateaus were his low-gravity stairwell. He spiraled his way downward, into the dark, ever downward, the blood marbles coalescing into the size of a basketball.

A shock and his frame convulsed to the edge of seizure. But the music was closer, pressing his organs back into action, one soldier after another, slowly reporting for duty.

"Engage reviving fluids," he heard a familiar female voice say, and the darkness retook him.

This time he walked, his boots crunching against the gravel path. He felt the warm air from the breeze dance upon his cheek, and he hoped the breeze would still be there later to keep the bugs off the porch after dinner.

Arriving at his log cabin, Oswald saw a thin column of smoke emerging from the chimney. He sniffed the air, and his mouth started to water. His beloved wife was inside cooking dinner, and his newborn son was undoubtedly in there as well, being cute. Oswald couldn't wait to see them both. They were the lights of his life.

Before he could climb the steps to his porch, his chocolate lab burst around the corner. The dog sprinted, his tail wagging furiously and barking. When he arrived at his master, he stood on his hind legs, and Oswald let him lick his face. He calmed down his lab by scratching the scruff of the dog's neck.

Oswald bounced up the porch steps and walked inside. The last of the sunlight painted his wife and child in a shimmering column of light. Oswald couldn't help but feel fulfilled, like his life's goals were complete. What a night this was turning out to be.

His wife offered the child. "Take him while I finish dinner. He just woke up."

Oswald replied, "No problem," and he grabbed his boy. The baby cooed and reached for his father's short beard.

"Not this time. Those nails are sharp, buddy." Oswald held him at arm's distance as aggressive little hands swiped at his face. Just like his old man, he thought.

Oswald held the child at eye level and asked, "Were you good today? Did you behave for Mama?"

The baby just smiled and cooed. Oswald's wife stirred the pot. "He was a perfect little angel."

"Smells good," he said. "What are we having?"

She smirked. "Your favorite, of course."

The syncopated cacophony of the jazz approached. And what was Oswald's favorite meal, exactly? Steak? Stew? Soup? He couldn't remember. What was his wife's name, again? Or his child? It was all on the tip of his tongue.

At that moment, the world shook, and the illusion came apart. The roof detached from the house and flew up into the sky. The logs from the cabin tumbled and rolled down the grassy hill into the creek.

The faces of his wife and child were fading. Maybe if he remembered their names, he could stay. Oswald scrambled for a way to keep himself in this world. Perhaps it would help if he remembered his own.

Richard? Raj? What was his first name? It was something with an "R." Details were lost in the thaw.

Everyone in the barracks called him Oswald, and his family was among the system's very wealthiest. Some say money talks but wealth whispers. And his family whispered the softest. He couldn't quite remember what they did (rock collecting?) or for whom he fought. Maybe he fought for all of them. He usually joined whatever theater had the hottest action. He was sowing his oats, and he was good at it. It was something only the super-wealthy could do without fear of consequence.

Debt crushed him: an eye-popping, bone-chilling, monster-load of debt.

The powers-that-be declared participation in the war to be a war crime. Not that the fighting stopped. But every action had a price dictated by the market. From parking tickets to battlefield manslaughter, every cause had an effect. And there was no effect he couldn't afford, for a time.

***

His chest rocked with another violent spasm, and he imagined another fight. This time, Oswald was flying, gliding over the metallic methane sea. The rings in the sky, looming like the floating platform for heaven, told him he was near Saturn. Titan, probably.

From above, he saw the green of the floating colonies strung together. Their skinny grow houses looked like the stem of a rose, and the red community dome was the blossom. From this height, it was beautiful. He knew that red was the hub, where the most enemies would be, so he shot his arm-mounted weapons. Before his rockets exploded, their missiles responded, roaring towards Oswald. Everything hit at once, and he fell, crashing and drowning, dragged underneath by the silvery cling. Cold, always the cold, pressurized from above by memories and below by debt.

But this time, the cold broke, defeated by the be-bop or perhaps the big band. Oswald coughed, shivered, and choked himself alive. He couldn't open his eyes yet, so he just listened to a melodic female voice.

"Robert John Oswald, you have accumulated 399 trillion credits in personal debt, of which 48% has been paid, leaving 207 trillion, 48 billion...."

Oswald tuned out after the relief of hearing his first name was Robert. And that money was still counted in credits. He was old enough to remember dollars.

Some people had to fight in the wars, conscripted, and tried to incur as little debt as possible, laying low until their stint was over. But Robby went looking for violence, knowing he had no consequence. He owed the families of every person he killed in his wars compensation.

It wasn't that Oswald was an evil person. War was part of the family business. He still hated his father, flat out loathed the man. As a boy, his dad would creep up and rock his jaw with a couple of hooks. There were no jabs. Everything was a power punch. Maybe it was supposed to toughen him up and remind him that the fight could start at any time. He didn't know.

The killing started as a way to shame the family, perhaps bankrupt his father. But as his notoriety grew, Oswald suspected his father only grew prouder of him. His boy was on the front lines of the age-old war between capital and labor. Every enemy Oswald smote carried his father's pasty grinning approval.

The tech greeted Oswald as he woke. "There he is," she said. "Everyone's favorite space miner that went broke."

Space Mining. That's how his family earned their fortune. The eldest son, the scion, set to inherit the system and all the treasures within. His crimes didn't even dent the family's capital.

It was, of all things, the free market that made them a pauper. When a rival mining company mastered the ability to tow rocks into near-Moon orbit, the price for rare materials crashed.

When Oswald saw a solid gold asteroid circling the moon, it was the most beautiful sight he'd ever witnessed. For the Oswald family and their key shareholders, it meant total financial ruin.

"Dreaming of the Elementals?" the tech said, unable to keep the wonder from her voice. Oswald was a founding member of the mercenary group. Their wood-paneled yacht club was prohibitively expensive, as were the mech suits. But funding in the name of violence, his father didn't mind.

Each wealthy investor constructed mechs. They loaded the suits with the best technology society could offer and styled them after slots in the periodic table.

Other founders picked hard metals like Iron. This was a reference to an old song or movie, maybe both. Those warriors who wore Iron would waste time telling him all about it. Of course, Platinum and Gold were popular choices. He shared battles with a half dozen Gold-79's during his decade-long terror run. And like their namesakes, Golds often proved soft. One murderous redhead took Ar-33 for Arsenic, the most notorious poisons. She was fast, but she never touched Oswald's rank on the leaderboards.

Oswald was Carbon-6, famous for being among the building blocks of life. But among those blocks, one could also find the keys to death inside. Carbon was versatile. It didn't have to be a diamond-tipped bullet to kill. Any amount could be deadly, given the correct dosage. Oxygen gives us life but combined with a straightforward Carbon, and it becomes Carbon Monoxide, a deadly poison. Add another, and it's Carbon Dioxide. Too much carbon dioxide in the blood was a common risk for those in cryostasis. There were a million ways to kill with Carbon. Science probably discovered a couple more while he was on ice.

He looked down at the orange panels of his suit, the armor lying around him like the remains of a hatched bird's egg. He saw pinstripes, smiley faces and old corporate logos he didn't recognize. More compensation to lower his debt, to be sure. The stickers covered notches, notably the lines he carved into the upper arm gauntlets, recording his body count.

The suit was a powered exoskeleton that wove its way into Oswald's bones. It offered him super strength, and the retractable arm cannons could swap between bullets, lasers, and small guided missiles.

Yet, for as much death he could deal, the real tricks were inside the helmet. The neuro-detection fed him constant data. He could read the thought patterns of every human or animal within a hundred-meter range.

They hadn't gotten to his chest plate yet. Besides being weapons of mass destruction, the suits were also self-contained suspended animation pods. Nano-slime drifted to localized problem areas. Anaerobic delivery prevented muscle atrophy while he slept. At least he didn't have to add pod-rental to his massive debt. That's where they really got you.

How long was he fighting? Physically, he was still a healthy young man, only in his early thirties. He fought ten tours in total. Oswald would never forget the lavish ceremony the other Elementals threw him, renting out the main hall of a pleasure station off Mercury. Behind the tempered glass, he watched the sun swirl. That memory kept him warm. But it was long ago.

"Where's Arsenic?" Oswald asked, daring to open his eyes. Tubes were feeding and draining him. "33? She was here last time."

"Paid her debt," the tech said. "Last time I saw her, she bought the cheapest ticket to anywhere out of system flying steerage."

"Good for her," Oswald mumbled. Maybe there was a way out of debt for some. Probably not for him.

"Given the logos, gallery ticket sales, your debt is predicted to be paid in..." the tech trailed off.

"Shoot," she muttered, looking Oswald in the eyes for the first time. "Do you even want to know?"

Oswald shook his head. It had to be centuries. "What's your name, again, tech?" he asked.

"Jaide," she said. "Every time with this." Pretty name. Was it common? Had it gone out of style and come back again? How many times had she told him this? He wouldn't know.

"Jaide, let's help each other out. When can I go back under?" he asked. It was all the hope he could muster. Perhaps he'd run into a pleasant delusion, like the log cabin, shuffled in among all the poisonous ones.

"You know we're supposed to wait here for half a day," Jaide said with a sigh. "Eat a meal, workout, maybe." But that meant she would have to wait as well, and the glimmer in her eye told Oswald everything he needed to know.

Jaide furiously forged the records, gesturing approval for all the nonexistent procedures they didn't run.

"Before you put me back down, can you look something up for me? Did I have a wife?"

"Every time," Jaide said, shaking her head. "I don't have to look it up. You never got married. But a few thaws ago, we found your engagement announcement to one Abigail Cairn. Her family was loaded, just like yours. But she broke it off after, ya know, all the murders."

Abigail. Abby. Her name recalled their last vacation together: the citrus-vanilla breeze through the palm trees over the Grand Wailea beach.

He went mute. There was no log cabin or baby, but Abby was real. She was beautiful, kind, and intelligent. Too bright to marry the system's most infamous war-killer.

"There's a whole crowd out there, you know," she said. "Just like every other day. Waiting to see the inert man in his murderous suit."

"Well," he said, empty of emotion. "It would be a shame to disappoint them."

It was a win-win for both of them. The tech would get paid for a half-day off, and Oswald would get whatever small portion of the daily gate he would have missed eating synthetic bacon and eggs. He'd be that much closer to freedom, that much closer to his revenge. And more importantly, he wouldn't have to live through the boredom of actual life.

* * *

The cold was again settling into his bones as they positioned him on the museum stage. It wasn't much of a museum, more of a fueling rest-stop on the way out of the system. But it had a few notable pieces, such as Carbon-6, a cautionary tale of unpaid debt. He rotated very slowly, giving his eye camera different views while on ice.

"Welcome to the Gallery of Yesterday," the tech's bored voice intoned over the speakers.

"In this exhibition, there are several paintings," the tech read. "The Merry Jesters, by Henri Rousseau, Nude Descending a Staircase by Marcel

Duchamps, and Flowers in a Vase, by Claude Monet. Of course, the log cabin landscapes of legendary painter Bob Ross need no introduction. These works are on long-term loan from the Philadelphia Museum of Art, all the way from Earth itself."

Jaide was probably supposed to read that last part with some enthusiasm, perhaps an exclamatory, but she stopped short as if expecting far more text in the script.

While the liquid iced him down, Oswald received an alert from his neuro-intelligence systems. The dominant lense scanned the crowd, highlighting a teenage boy. It identified his brain pattern as familial. Within a statistical amount of certainty, the suit could determine that this boy was his direct descendant.

The baby in the cabin. Was Abigail pregnant? The freezing quickened, and he felt himself losing the thread. His last action was to will his camera focus toward the boy, specifically, the eye of the boy. The teenager looked concerned as if he wanted to help Oswald.

There's nothing you, or anyone, can do for me, Oswald thought. He willed his cam to zoom further in-depth into the boy's eye: brows, lashes, the whites, then the iris. Microscopic into the web of brown, he plunged.

Oswald emerged in deep blackness fighting around the asteroid Ceres, explosions sending him spiraling into the vacuum of space.

The stars swirled, surrounding him in all directions as he dodged wispy rust-colored energy beams nearing his suit. He armed his system, turned on the jets, and killed, just like he always did—the jazz was only another memory, long since receded into the void.

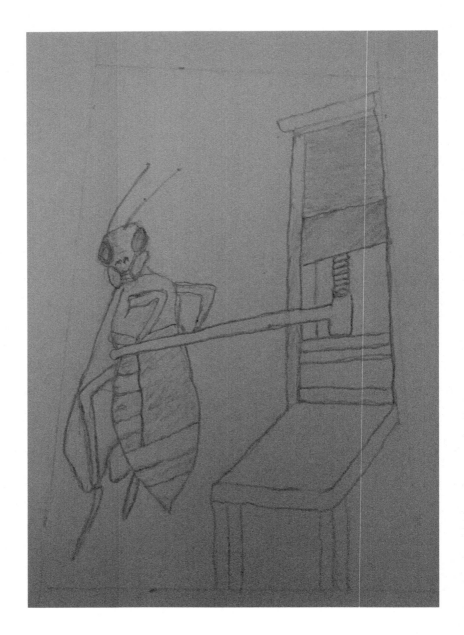

"Frankford Press" by Robert V. Kilroy

A Landfill Adventurer's Guide

by Robert V. Kilroy

Robert Frost published Fire and Ice in the December 1920 edition of Harpers.

One hundred years to the month the pandemics started, almost like fulfilling a contract with a demon.

December 2020 saw the death of a living document. The United States was the first to stumble. Without a villain to blame, warlords become CEOs, giving rise to the obscenely wealthy. Blood sacrifice was in vogue again, giving rise to the temperature, giving rise to the new gods, corporations.

Humanity tried to make a stand, like characters in a Tolkien novel without a ring to save them. Fragments of a planet-killing asteroid rained down on those who could least afford to protect themselves. Once great cities became instant landfills.

The floodwaters baptized every coastline throughout the globe. Governments collapsed almost as fast. Tribalism was reborn. When the mighty tower fell, six Babels rose to meet the people's needs, not so much regional as ideological; they adopted the colors of the rainbow for distinction: Red and Blue, then Yellow, Orange, Purple and Green.

Like the floodwater, everything found its new level. No job, no problem. The true age of socialism dawned. Food, shelter, and Reality TV were all the Stoner/Donor class required. Jobs were abundant for those who were raised to have a purpose.

All the world became a stage.

The corporate camera droids appeared over the receding waters, making endless content for content's sake. So many that the buzzing must have sounded like mosquitoes. Humanity officially embraced the lives of the insects. The hum was here to stay.

Now some of the population will always be more adventurous. Treasure hunting became so popular the young chose it for their stage.

If corporations were gods, the billionaires who profited were at least demi-gods. These would-be gods realized the golden age of larping had arrived. A lucrative industry, all the dungeons without the dragons. Many of the mega rich earned their first dollar as gamers. Why wouldn't they leap at the chance to bring their monsters to life?

The trash adventurers were born.

WINTER'S SOLSTICE

Staring, thinking and reflecting.

His final shift on the most dangerous service job the Red caps had to offer. Vanguard Mining Engineer or glorified ditch digger, Winter advanced through every challenge the corporation had to offer. He would now be fast-tracked off this rotting work camp known as earth. Like a foreigner who served in the Roman army for 20 years, he was eligible for full citizenship: he could get the operation, Crystal blue optical implants. Total immersion into Aryan society could not be complete without the blue eyes.

Hiding his disgust for the system was his true occupation. Some still carried the genetic natural defect that almost tore the ancient world apart; Winter endured being passed over time and time again because of his grandparents' ocular sins. Watching virtual idiots crash and burn for the sake of a lie. Mandatory organ donation was the agreement they made to wear the engineering suit. If a suit malfunctioned, the medics didn't race to save lives as much as to preserve an underachieving legacy's blue eyes. These treasured orbs would be forwarded to a more deserving candidate. A Frankenstein society.

Winter was extraordinarily smart and had a plan. Never an accident. He learned every engineering course those ignorant bastards offered. He proved to be a proper corporate investment, a natural in the tech suit. It seemed the more complicated the tool, the more symbiotic he was.

For someone 100% Biological, his quest to touch the gods had finally arrived. His natural brown hues never hurt him physically. Growing up in the shadow of the Red space elevator, Winter knew the simple color of his eyes would never afford him access. Now eligible for blue, he could immediately pay for the upgrade to the lithium processor, and skip having to see through the eyes of a dead co-worker. Only full Aryan citizens were eligible for their tech.

Trading his eyes, not for a better job or even status, a bluff he had crafted for years: going full cyborg was perceived as "all in" acceptance to the Ivy League, a cushy career off planet.

Head in the Cloud.

This effectively connected him to everything knowable.

Forget their aristocracy.

He would be in control of his life.

The downside of never again being allowed to participate in any casino games was a small price to pay, even though he used that vehicle to amass the small fortune needed for ascension. The company never lost. They would simply provide contests among participants while skimming from the top; those blue light emitting diodes would test opponents with each bet. Outwitting his co-workers from their futures had grown old.

Still a gambler, only now a bigger game.

Leaving the salt flats of Utah was necessary for him to grow his empire and self-respect. Wanderlust is the true calling of an adventurer.

When the bandages were removed his Little Eric got hard, rebooting faster than anyone the medical team had ever seen. The Wizard was born.

No goodbyes, hospital to airport. Without a word, Winter boarded the shuttle east and never looked back.

Listening to a barrage of bigotry and personal questions from the Red-capped medical sales representative seated across from him, who seemed to be falling for his pretty blue eyes, Winter finally spoke. "Madam, I'd rather be in Philadelphia."

DOORA GETS THE START

A female athlete works her whole life for success and respect. She must be the total package. Strength, intelligence, and charisma doesn't hurt when you're finally given the ball.

This wasn't Doora's first adventure in front of the camera. She had cut her teeth as a torch and load bearer, support cast member. Her ability to forget the cameras and spin genuine banter in the face of danger gave her quite the following. The sideshow never interested her. Solving traps was her forte.

Entertaining a labyrinth of waste, death, and failed consumerism had become Reality TV. The squad Doora fronted was called Team Gilgamesh, a professional adventurers' party with more than 50,000 paid subscribers. Like any sport, fans watched Doora to share in her victories while fearing a violent clash, and here the players could die or worse, in real time.

Most dungeon entrances were enormous, twenty foot around, before gradually closing down to ten or five. These sizes became industry standard, the industry of raw materials extraction. Imagine gargantuan metallic mosquitoes whose proboscis repeatedly pierced Mother Earth. These tubes could continue for miles. The extraction sent the raw material to the 'thorax' where the molecular analysis and separation occurred, keeping the desired materials in the 'abdomen' and expelling the waste, creating a gray hilly terrain.

When unorganized adventurers started sifting through these man-made foothills they gained the name goblins: too adventurous for the service industry, yet needing more than socialism could offer. The godless goblins usually stayed clear of spelunking and simply panhandled with sifters and magnets. Being labeled goblin was a stereotype not necessarily criminal.

Orcs on the other hand could prove quite lethal. This name was given to the unsponsored who simply took what they wanted. Bounties were paid for these claim jumpers. Lawlessness didn't last long. Bounty hunters had their own networks. Cameras were everywhere. And so it went.

Deeper and deeper through the semi-petrified filth path Doora dragged her sled, which she named Rosebud. The walls, ceilings and floors were coated with a plastic residue left behind by the once-thriving corporate leviathans. This glaze allowed the probes to be efficiently maneuvered in and out of the newly created orifices in the violated earth, a bizarre casing where the sausage was on the outside. Once the heated probes were removed, the translucent viscous lode would cool, leaving a passage. This procedure was the secret to creating modern dungeons, like visiting an aquarium and finding only dead capitalism.

Doora peered at the map she had strapped to her forearm. The ten-foot hallway continued with occasional smaller branches all around. Doora's exit was a five-foot-wide opening marked with medical waste containers. Tracking the signs like posters for an underground rave, the opening expanded to a larger chamber filled with alarming, bright red biomedical bags.

One hundred feet over Doora's head, an old man lounged in the cab of a repurposed corporate troop transport, staring at the luminous spider's silk tungsten cables, which wound the wench disappearing into the abandoned mine entrance and provided her only way out. They were in what was left of the once thriving suburb of Northern Philadelphia where the floodwaters were long gone, having burned off in this compost pit.

Once a front-line adventurer risking life and limb for glory and treasure, the old man, Fagan, now organized a younger generation of adventurers. Having experience and modest success from his previous life, he ran his own low level extraction business. Being a guild member in good standing with proper paperwork, Fagan was afforded protections the godless scabs could never enjoy. The Guild gave Fagan access to tools, weapons, registered adventurers, and most importantly, Quests.

He felt a familiar pain sting the two remaining stained and blistered fingers on his biological right arm: the poor excuse for a Salem had burned down again, returning his gaze to darkness.

His guild ticket read Cleric 5th Class, but many cards were hidden behind the aged plastic badge. Technology allowed Fagan to lead from the rear after his mind and body were no longer able.

The click-click-click from the deep sea rig came to an abrupt stop, snapping Fagan from his trance. His eyes flashed to the monitor that received images from Doora's body camera.

Licking partially burned lips, he issued his command. "Stop right there!"

Doora's angry reply came through the speaker. "Stop yellin' at me!"

"What do you see?"

"Red biohazard bags. The whole area is covered with them like wallpaper."

"You still got your glove on?"

"This is a gauntlet not a glove! The book says keep your armor on at all times."

"All it is, is a hindrance! Now take the Trumpin' glove off and start squeezing the bags! Let me know when you find a squishy one."

"You're nuts!"

Fagan tried to gather himself and respond like the elder he was. "You still have ten pinkies, anything goes wrong, you can upgrade! Now do as I say and find me the juiciest bag."

Doora listened to her team leader and removed the gauntlet, poking a finger into each bag. Much to her surprise, they were relatively dry. After minutes of silence, she was amazed to find the old man's prediction to be true.

"I found it."

"You've only just begun," responded the Cleric in a soothing and melodic tone. "Take off your mask and tell me what the contents of the bag smell like."

"What is wrong with you? First off, the book says an adventurer never removes her helmet while adventuring. And secondly, this place probably smells like butt!"

"You're going to need to taste it."

"That is definitely a 'no go' in the handbook!"

"Listen to me and listen good. You are on a Quest that has led us beyond your entry level. I am impressed you read the damn text, but your handbook is only a guide. You are too cautious. Stretch your abilities within the parameters of your chosen class. Much is required of you. A thief can do it all. Why do you think I pulled this Quest for you? This mine has been picked over by more experienced adventurers with better tech. The party that cleared this level left markers for the treasures they never exhumed."

"Are you finished?"

"Is your torchbearer awake?"

Listening to the old man's rambling, the young adventurer almost forgot she wasn't alone in the pit. The torchbearer connected to her tow line was happy to have a job outside the service industry. Holding the powerful light source almost made him invisible below the 360 degrees of the piercing luminous sphere.

"Hey Shadows, are you with me?"

"My name is Blake."

"Shadows sounds better."

"Are you really going to take your helmet off?"

"Fagan said it was part of my education. Besides, you're here to save me, right?"

"If you say so."

Fagan interrupted. "Enough Trumpin' chatter on the line! Get that helmet off now and tell me what you smell."

Lifting the visor, the light grabbed her before any odor. "It smells like musty humid trash."

"The bag! The bag! What do you smell?"

"It smells like plastic."

Not being down in the hole with the young ones was starting to wear on the old man. "You need to smell the contents of the bag."

"You're serious? That red biohazard bag is sealed for a reason."

"TAKE YOUR KNIFE OUT AND CUT THE BAG OPEN."

Like a failed saving throw for a Command spell, Blake reached out from the shadow under the glowing orb and with one swift motion split the bag with his Bowie. Lucky for the man, his partner took the contents of the squishy sack and not himself. The dark red fluid of the biohazard bag splattered on Doora like Sissy Spacek's prom night.

"I'll kill you!" Doora spat the liquid that drained from her saturated head.

Fagan asked, "What do you taste? Focus, Doora, what do you taste?"

She allowed her brain to receive and process the message from her assaulted taste buds. "Raspberry jam."

"You found it! You did it! You found it!" His words of positive reinforcement almost immediately defused her urge to gut the torchbearer.

"What just happened?" She continued to wipe the fructose from her face.

"You found the marked wall. Now carefully start to remove the bags behind that wall."

"This is the hall of records? How do you know?"

"The Quest is only ever spoken. I was trying to give you the background and you interrupted me."

Doora cleared the mess from her head and shoulders as Fagan continued.

"When the high-level adventurers emptied the valuable tech and resources, they also found some specialty items they hid for later. Anything brought up would have been confiscated under the original contract. By hiding and mapping the find, they could sell the map of their discovery to younger adventurers who might reap the true market value for a specific collector. I only hope it is the collection from the legend."

Using their shovels, picks, and brushes the treasure hunters began to make cautious progress towards the hidden riches.

"Why use the bag of jelly?"

"These abandoned mines are not foolproof from scabs. Unless you have some training, the sight of red biohazard bags will keep away the uncleansed from fear of something infectious."

After what felt like hours of meticulous scratching and removing sediment, the remaining wall fell forward, revealing its contents. Like the ancient archaeologists who first unearthed Tutankhamun, they found themselves face to face with a smirking alien ancestor.

Blake shouted two words, "Bill Cosby!" Blake knew that face from the Ancient Offender Studies class he had taken in his previous career in law enforcement.

The now unearthed chamber revealed a set of plastic totable cases. Opening just a few revealed a collection that would make the team the talk of the camp: century-old comedians on vinyl. Moms Mabley, George Carlin, Robin Williams, Shelley Berman, Lenny Bruce, Richard Pryor, Redd Foxx, Eddie Murphy, Don Rickles, Woody Allen, Lily Tomlin, Sam Kinison, Jackie Mason, Freddie Prinze, and Rodney Dangerfield to name more than a few. When the last of the cases was removed, the count stood at 273 albums, all still in their jackets. A true haul of records.

THE RIDE HOME

Having secured the treasures from this "dive," Fagan recalled his surveillance drones for charging. Using his own drones to run interference allowed him to control the content team Gilgamesh released to their adoring audience. You might say he was the executive producer of the beloved circus. Fresh drones with charged batteries and ammunition took to formation as the formidable transport headed westward.

"I hope this comes out of my hair without a problem," grumbled Doora.

"Are you still belly-aching? When I'm done editing the footage you will get rookie of the month and 15,000 more followers!"

"Just get us home."

"I will, I will, but we need to swing by Quaker Town first."

"Don't tell me we're seeing going to see the Goblin."

"Yes, we're going to see Jonny G. I thought you liked him?"

"I love that he takes care of all the little goblins."

"Now, Jonny G isn't a monster. 'Matter of fact he's the second smartest sage I know after Mange. Speaking of Mange, when we get home I'm sure he has some product that will restore your beautiful locks."

"Enough already!"

Quaker Town was a misnomer; there hadn't been a Quaker there in half a century. It was however flush with goblins, essentially good people who just wanted to be left alone. Orcs learned quickly to avoid this territory.

The goblins were the embodiment of the Phillyamish militia, a classification of farmers and special forces not unlike the indigenous folk of the region, a tight-knit community of like-minded, god-fearing people who loved and supported their neighbors. This militia was important for the success of the thriving goblin community, which hosted their training grounds. Phillyamish hit back, hard. Not formally organized, but as long as most could remember, Fagan's friend Jonny G was their unofficial governor, the closest thing to royalty these uncleansed masses would ever know.

Doora said, "Don't tell me the Hobgoblin is going to be there, too."

"You know I have to check in on the community. Besides, I thought you liked visiting all the kids the Goblin King is raising out here."

"I love seeing the children."

"Lucky for you we don't have time for an extended stop over."

"Now I get it. You packed a few pallets of company goods. So you're the one running the black market out here?"

"Run? No. Support? Of course. How do you suppose we stay on top? The basement is different from your ivory tower my little princess. Jonny G is the man who gets things done in Quaker Town."

"If you're telling me we can leave as soon as we unload this stuff, I will be glad to help speed things along."

"Sounds good to me. Just don't commit to playing any games with the young un's."

"Baby goblins are adorable."

Anyone who wanted to participate in this agricultural lifestyle would be accepted. Modest modular homes made up the lion's share of domiciles in this territory. More Flintstones than Jetsons.

The houses were more densely populated as they approached his compound. The big goblin loved to be with the people; he did however enjoy his privacy. His McMansion was high on the area's working quarry. This was more of a cover story than a resource. The surrounding homes all had elaborate tunnels that would make the Viet Cong jealous.

Once Fagan entered the Goblin King's compound, he maneuvered his transport around to a sizable Quonset hut.

Before the backside ramp hit the ground, scores of goblins surrounded the transport like a rock star's tour bus. Some had already began soaping up and hosing the sediment left from the dungeon. Still others were removing containers, packages, and cables. Most were young and wanted to touch and catch a glimpse of Doora, the new "it girl."

"Go and meet your adoring public. I'll keep the King busy."

Doora obliged and temporarily left the foul taste she had been harboring.

As Fagan exchanged invoices and papers with the garage master from his driver's seat window, he could see and hear the Goblin King approach.

"Faaaagan, my good friend."

Even though this reality of adventurers was more scavenger and Hollywood make-believe, Jonny had the ability to "charm person" by stretching out your name when greeting.

"Jonny! Can't stay long, my King. The prophecies are afoot!"

With that, Jonny soberly responded, "Do you have time to thank the Gods and help me with this 'fatty'?" He revealed a long, finger-sized blunt.

"I always have time to thank the Gods with your burnt offerings," Fagan responded politely.

The King whisked around the front of the vehicle and entered the cab.

"What's with the long robes and turban?" Fagan asked, crushing a Salem and lighting the chronic.

"Just trying to play my part for the kids." He took a mighty puff. "Should we get in the hot tub?"

"Sorry, no time."

"I understand. Next time you bring your librarian friend with you, warn me. It took me a week to get his hair out of the drain."

With that Fagan started to cough and lose his smoke.

Jonny said, "You know I love the little guy. As a matter of fact, I acquired a handful of graphic novels by Miller. I remember he likes to unwind with the classics."

"He will appreciate that. Speaking of, he believes our little project is ready."

With that, Jonny coughed up a cloud of offering.

Fagan continued, "I have many of the components to jump start your throne."

Jonny G, glassy eyed, lamented, "It's all coming together so fast. You said it would. I really thought this day was just talk and hyperbole. I don't want to lose you."

"All this is necessary for our survival. I'm sure your spies have been warning you for awhile now. We did the math over and again; it's time."

Crushing out the roach, Jonny continued, "Sonny confirmed there was troop movement from the west when he delivered his last shipment of chronic to those Red hat assholes. You know they talk a big game, but they can't hold their smoke. They canceled their next order. That could only mean they expect to be here to collect for themselves. I thought he was being paranoid."

"More like when dogs know an earthquake is going to hit. So you're ready for the exodus?"

Still looking down at the ashes with a look of concern, Jonny said, "We're ready."

"Don't be sad, my King. The girl needs to survive, and I must fulfill my destiny. It's not like they'll crucify me. Once they collect and the numbers check out, case closed!"

"You only live once, my brother."

Fagan squinted with a wry smile.

WELCOME TO SECOND CITY

Bob Marley echoed through the streets of old Allentown when the Mayflower returned from a successful campaign. Like Pavlovian dogs, half the residents broke out in song and cheered as if Haile Selassie himself had returned. Those that didn't celebrate were too focused on videogames or Reality TV.

New Allentown was now the Pennsylvania east coast destination. Disaster brings change; technology makes it palatable. Enormous 3D-printers allowed planners to start over. Think of it as an elevated or raised society. A stacked chessboard. Translucent steel they called it. Not really steel, but it was still Allentown. The building trades hit the ground running. An entire metropolis on stilts to avoid the next flood. Opportunities abound.

The protein zombie phenomenon never gained a foothold in the Quaker state. With so many abandoned mines in the region, the waters receded quickly. Good news: the Centralia mine fires were finally out. We still had outlying farmlands for exporting, but now urban gardens were the norm. Like Babylon on steroids. Everywhere the sun shown it was employed, absorbed or reflected. Hunger was no more.

Old real estate was cheaper, allowing Fagan to build quite the influential compound. Two square city blocks formed the base of this mighty ziggurat. Each level consisted of a weaving of solar panels and various foliage. The centerpiece was the downtown firehouse, one of many societal 'goodies' Fagan provided. He felt fulfilled like Caesar returning from Gaul whenever he passed under those great arches.

No time to rest. Doora raced to the shower, Blake retreated to the mosque.

The old man had a date at the Brokerage House. Using his six-wheeler, he climbed the old federal building steps that now housed the guild complex. Snipers, 30 millimeters, and guardsmen smiled as he entered the massive structure to meet the Deputy Minister.

"Fagan, the prophet of profit! You've done it again. More than half of your treasures are sold and those that remain are stuck in a bidding war."

"You embarrass me, Deputy Minister."

"You mean, I know you, old man. No one else is even close to your success rate. Especially when it comes to off-planet Quests. You must have a direct communal to the deities themselves."

"It would seem that your old habits are hard to die as well there, DM. When you ran these streets for me, you were the tops in information retrieval. You've done well for yourself."

"Guilty, my friend. You are the one who can come into this market and pick the rights to these projects like picking the ripest melon. I am jealous is all. I guess I just miss the action."

"You have the noblest profession in this chaotic world. Like the mayor of Eden after the apple incident."

They both chuckled.

Fagan continued, "You have ensured the order and integrity that is lacking in other regions of our adventurous society. We are now drawing some of the best recruits. Speaking of . . . don't you have a fresh work card for me to squeeze?"

"Now this is getting scary. How can you possibly know that?"

"You know I don't normally commune and tell, but I will make an exception for you my old friend. He or she is an 'unspoiled' wizard of the west, a recent recipient of the famed optical engineering. They give off an ever so slight beacon. Tell me, was he wearing sunglasses throughout his interview process, no?"

"As a matter of fact he was. And I was surprised he responded to my Cory Hart reference. Astonishing!"

"Don't get too carried away there, Casey Kasem. He is a Red team runaway. He is legally tapped into the cloud. It won't be long before they attempt to retrieve someone like himself who has dared to leave the reservation. I am going to need some dampeners for him. The last thing we need is some crusade of those red-capped psychos trying to retrieve their 'lost' electric sheep before we find out if he can still dream."

"You Dick!"

"No, you the Dick!" They loved the classics, both giggling like schoolboys. "We will need individual as well as portable area dampeners. I am also going to need the best tech suit you can lay your hands on. All the bells and whistles for digging. Also, your latest catalog for the rest of the team. This kid, if I'm right, will put your operation on the world stage when I'm done with him. This would-be adventurer is what I have been waiting for."

Meanwhile outside, Winter sat cross-legged on a courtyard lunch table admiring the steps of the pyramid just across the wide avenue. He counted 13 levels that broke through the dividing translucent ceiling of Old Allentown, six floors below and seven above. Above, the pyramid shined like a star, covered in solar panels. The levels below however seemed to be double floors. The area he calculated was immense for an urban development. This was the semi-famous (at least in the adventurers' guides) Gilgamesh Project. A world unto itself. Winter wanted in.

He observed dozens of workers on each level of the mega structure. Armed guards sprinkled the landscape, only detected by his special optics. His newly connected synapses were firing at a frantic pace to come up with the perfect interview responses for the legendary old man. Spying on him as he entered the equally menacing keep behind him known as the Ministry of Adventurers, he could hear the Old Man's six-wheeler long before he emerged from the great hallway. Much to his astonishment, the metallic Drow Lord veered to his table, only resting when parallel to him.

Before the unemployed adventurer could speak, the old man asked, "Are you a good man?"

"I've never been accused of being a do-gooder. Then again, I've never felt compelled to label someone else. So I must be. I have been a solitary scholar. An autodidact perhaps? My understanding of good faith is, do it in the dark. Your light only identifies itself in the absence of such things. The world as I see it, is suffering a perpetual glomming. Not too dark and not too bright. More of the latter. I do think we can do better. We must. Hoarding was the motto of Philadelphia. Call it Liberty all you want, a broken bell is trash until recycling day."

"Oh, before we start, you need to put on this ring."

Winter looked at the spartan piece of jewelry, analyzing as he accepted and complied.

"You skipped out on your exit interview with the Reds."

"What do you mean?"

"The last task is that 'optional' light bright cube they had you perform on. My guess is you picked up and strolled out of the hospital before inadvertently entering their electronic contractual cage. You must be damn good at what you do because they assumed you were joining the cult off planet. You had to have walked away from an absurd commission. They would have had a lesser candidate under armed supervision. You fooled them but good. Make no mistake, they don't let their tech wander off. You may think you found a loophole. They will come for those baby blues. This ring will dampen the signal you're giving off."

Winter thought, I'm not the wisest guy in the room. Finally! "So, what now?"

"We go and meet your new family. You can start by sprucing up our electrical systems, including my squeaky wheels."

"That's a job for WD-40."

"Then you will teach that to your little brothers and sisters."

Winter took to this language of positive inclusion; it was inspiring.

"Try some of these berries."

Having crossed the avenue and traversed half the block, Fagan came to an abrupt stop.

"The berries around the perimeter."

Winter realized the eccentric old man referred to the gargantuan hedgerows hiding the iron gates of Gilgamesh. He reached in, avoiding the thorny thickets. "These are amazing! But I can't really identify the fruit I am tasting."

"This is the mana that draws in the lost ones to our cause."

"And what is our ultimate cause?"

"Why, self-actualization, of course. These abandoned and forsaken youths of Old Allentown. My children."

"How many are we talking about?"

"Hundreds over the years."

Winter wondered if he left one cult only to join another.

"Come on Winter, I have been waiting for you for years. Someone clever enough to escape the Reds with your special abilities. You obviously don't want to be part of the endless civil war with the Blues. You want to be allowed to self-actualize. I can't go on forever. You need us as much as I need you. You are going to be my successor."

"Wo, a little fast, aren't you?"

"I needed someone to complete my ultimate party. A lawful good wizard."

"You really believe in all this live action role playing, don't you?"

"All the world's a stage. Besides, if you were nefarious, you would have went right to the Blue."

Winter had never met anyone who seemed to be two steps ahead like this character. They passed under the great arch, Winter thinking he needed to get one of these horseless chariots. The pause that Winter had been experiencing since the implants was broken by the noisy chariot of his benefactor pulling away. "Are you coming?"

"Yes, Winter's coming."

Crossing the threshold of the First Level was disorienting to the newly crowned Green wizard. Winter wasn't new to the gigantic hangers of the Red work camps of Utah. This was different. His hearing was suddenly drowning. The squeaking of the old man's six-wheeler was suffocated, probably why no one in the garage noticed. This was not the soundtrack of a world class service center. The walls of this leviathan were consuming all sound. A different world, more like a church. The metallic spine rose in the center with elevators, stairs, and humongous chases. They entered a smaller lift and exited the second floor labeled Library.

Fagan asked, "Mange, where are you at?"

"By the new books you just acquired."

The voice came from the direction they had just been. The sound of the words were easily understood, not like on the floor below; more of the 'looking glass,' thought Winter. This understanding could not prepare him for the next wandering monster. Glasses adorned the pleasant voiced werewolf, who approached reading a first edition hardbound medical textbook. Mange the Librarian (Dean of the Forsaken) suffered from hypertrichosis.

Fagan said, "Now Mange, there is no excuse for you to smell as bad as me. I've been out adventuring and you've been drinking books like an alcoholic on a borrowed liver! Come meet our friend, Winter the wizard."

The hoarder ladened corridor of books smelled of equal parts classics and sweet body odor.

"Winter, I have been reading up on your precious gifts. They really are as blue as the manual says." Mange slowly closed the book.

Winter jumped in, "Your yellow eyes are quite formidable themselves my friend."

"Of course you could see this isn't jaundice but rather the knock-off Air-Jordan's in my sockets. I would love to play you in a game of chess!"

Fagan chortled, "No time you smelly cur. Take a shower, eat a meal, then meet us in the boardroom on Five."

Mange seemed to snap from his waking fog to a more serious demeanor. "On Five? That serious, huh? I'll be there. Boss, your deliveries from Yellow Corp have arrived. Personnel are in the sub and the lad's suit is on Six by the chair."

"Good boy."

"Trump you, you poor excuse for a broken GI-Joe doll."

"That's more like it!"

Taking the elevator to the sixth floor, or the Throne Room as it were, Winter downloaded the pass codes and apps unlocking each level as he passed and was granted access. The doors opened to a spotless, computer laden clean room. There were a few sleeping tables but the chair was the obvious purpose of this level. Elevated, massive and encased behind some translucent protective barrier, not unlike the very ceiling of this undead city.

Moving to the bivouac allocation, Winter's processors began to consume the obvious brains of the mega complex, dozens of cables and exposed golden bus bars for moving electricity and information at speeds that would take the breath of an elder Swami.

Stopping at the casket closest to the 'show,' Fagan turned with a prideful smile. "I know you must have heard about the 'magic underpants' living in Salt Lake City."

A jumpsuit that through the eyes of the wizard seemed to be alive; Winter could hardly process the garment he was holding. "So this is the legendary vestment. Lighter than silk, stronger than Kevlar, and infused with healing nanotechnology."

"Yeah, pretty groovy, huh?"

"Groovy? How old are you?"

"Trump you, too. You would have been issued something like this if you accepted your commission with those ginger snaps."

Winter threw the garment on and it became form-fitting like a second skin. Never again would it need to be removed, if only for antiquated bathing rituals. He could feel the nanotechnology exfoliating the frailty of the human condition.

Fagan asked, "First time in the magical undies?"

"Yeah."

"Tingly huh?"

"Yeah, weirdly satisfying."

Following the old man around the shafts that delivered them to the throne room, Winter once again found himself near breathless.

"Is that what I think it is?"

Fagan nodded.

"Where did you get it?"

"Let's just say I have friends in the Yellow Corp that owe me."

Just outside the massive service elevator doors stood a hulk equally as impressive as the throne.

"A carbon processing excavating suit?"

"Oh boy, that would be like calling a nuclear battleship a boat. This is a prototype war machine. Digging is simply the cover story. I call it the 'Yellow Jacket.'"

Yellow and black bombarded the senses. Winter had worked in lesser suits his entire engineering life. This was something beyond even his highest level access in Red Corp. The armaments alone could take the top of the Gilgamesh ziggurat.

"We need to meet the rest of the team. You will have time to orient and play with your new toys. Off we go to Five."

MEANWHILE ON FIVE

The elders, the unofficial rulers of Old Allentown, waited for their leader. The massive table was made of 200-plus year-old African mahogany that had been thought extinct from its construction, a piece Fagan had 'picked up' whilst exploring the remains of the Hospital of the University of Penn; those surgeons really knew how to live it up.

Mange the Librarian, freshly groomed, was sitting alone with his head buried in multiple textbooks. Near the buffet tables to one side of the room stood three white-coated intellectuals, Scripture the Holy, Dr. Beatrix (for what ails you), and portly Cookie Dough the Dietitian. Across the room stood General Blake Salim, Colonel Barnabus, and Major Betty Rumble, living grim-faced Easter Island statues. Sitting next to each other yet emotionally worlds apart were Samuel the community liaison and Doora the Thief. The last visible member seated was Heather Goodheart, the assassin for peace; the coldest and most rational member remained focused on her treasured Sudoku puzzle.

The massive doors opened, causing all to quickly take their seats. Fagan and Winter moved to the far side head of the table. Flanking the old man, Winter couldn't help noticing an empty chair opposite his by Fagan's smoking hand. Fagan cavalierly whispered, "This seat is left for my Pooka, Harvey."

Curiously, this kind of one-way nonsensical exchange with Fagan was becoming easier to digest.

The old man addressed the room. "We knew this day would come. Still won't be any easier. The Red Caps are coming, soon. I take it we are ready, Barnabus?"

"When I got your call I deployed the Phillyamish."

Fagan nodded. "Samuel and Scripture, you need to start moving New Allentown residents to the shelters now. I feel this will not be a probe. They will be coming for blood. The bombs will be hitting like Dresden."

Scripture, a sizable man the likes of Tony Robbins, simply responded, "God is in his holy temple."

"Good, good." Swinging his head he faced the hybrid Amazon-Valkyrie. "Major, you have kept me safe longer than my expiration date. I now need you to shepherd our good Doctors through this, if we're going to keep this thing of ours alive."

"Understood," snapped Betty.

"General, Mange informs me our guests from Yellow Corp are in the basement waiting. You will lead them when the doors are breached. We need your faith like never before."

The paladin gestured silently, your words are in my mind, on my lips, and in my heart.

At this point Winter realized the woman at the far end of the table never raised her eyes from her puzzle book. His closer analysis caused him to blurt, "I know you!"

She slowly raised her head to gaze and respond. "Hey pretty blue eyes."

Continued Fagan, "All this hinges on your report my Bonny Heather."

"Winter and myself are the only survivors of the shuttle. That should have bought us a few hours at least." She returned to her puzzle book.

"Good, good, good. Doora you will take Winter up to the chair and wait for me."

Doora silently shook affirmative.

"My little birds tell me Red Corp will hit Blue, Yellow, and our lovely Green Lehigh Valley. We have tried to stay out of politics but hitting supply lines only makes tactical sense." Fagan fell into one of his vacant stares before pulling himself together with some self-deprecating laughter. "I'm no Lincoln, but I just realized that we're about four score years since those forefathers abandoned us when we needed them the most. They sold us on the duty to save humanity. They sailed away. We are once again left to the heavy lifting. Rebuilding society. We took an asteroid on the chin and survived. Those Blue coats are going to do what old Abe didn't have the stomach to do. Cut the Red head off the snake. History is trying to bury us as helpless martyrs. We must survive the sucker punch. That is what the Gilgamesh Project is about. SURVIVAL! We're not going to give up! We will work harder! Now take your positions."

Everyone started to exit the tension filled room. Doora, who never had an inside voice after the asteroid, turned to Winter. "Can I be Kelly to your Beyoncé in this Destiny's Child remix?"

All laughed, causing Fagan to holler, "That's my girl!"

When the room was vacant except two, Fagan opined to Mange, "I had hoped to be the Great Gatsby in this saga. Seems I'm merely Dr. TJ Eckleburg, I only get to watch from afar."

"Are you going to tell him?"

"That is my final responsibility."

THE WAR WILL NOT BE TELEVISED

The first explosions seemed distant from inside the mighty step pyramid; in reality they detonated only two-hundred or so meters above New Allentown. The deafening screeches brought down every drone like they were an ancient hero hearing a harpy's song. All video and reality programs went snowy. The Sixth Level of Gilgamesh was so insulated the blast went unnoticed.

The wizard and thief bonded immediately over observations of their broken benefactor.

Winter wondered, "How long have you been a ward of this crazy person?"

"You noticed already."

"Yeah, I'm a pretty quick study."

Doora paused then continued, "Since he found me in X-stasis. My memory was jumbled from the asteroid event."

"Are you telling me you are over eighty years old?"

"When you put it that way, you make a girl self-conscious for being ninety-three."

"Not at all. You are smoking hot!" Winter caught himself; somehow the new circuitry in the magical underpants caused him to blurt his emotional thoughts. "I am sorry for being so blunt and coarse. It's been the longest day of my life."

"Don't pull back now. I've been dealing with an unhealthy Daddy Warbucks complex since he pulled my sleeping 'egg' out of the rubble in Philadelphia. That's really all I remember. Doora isn't even my real name. My pod was damaged and the first thing I saw when I exited was the sign, Door-A. Then during my rehab, I realized I was as clueless as the animated girl with the monkey."

"Ah, the explorer."

"You got it."

"But why a thief?"

"Mange made me read the classics and I guess I identified with Oliver Twist. I don't think his real name is Fagan. I felt like I got the old man's joke. It was too late to change my name again to Olivia."

"Reinventing oneself for the better is the true secret power of this place."

"What about you? Why the quest for those dreamy eyes?"

Winter found it difficult to fight the nanotechnology in his suit when confronted with her banter. His answer came out like a confession. "I have no memory at all before my preteens as well. Headwound I guess? I chalked it up as a mixed blessing. I seemed to have an understanding most didn't or couldn't . . . ." Tears welled in his eyes.

"It's ok." The two virgins embraced, not knowing that the world was coming apart and the future of the universe was about to repeat. As they pulled apart, their faces close, she said, "I feel like we've known each other forever."

The Phillyamish held their positions as long as they could, but their AR-15s proved ineffective against the converted mining suits of the Red menace. The smart bombs that leveled the new city were only a grotesque misdirection. The Red troop transports closed around the besieged ziggurat.

The fire hydrants around this modern Alamo revealed their purpose, shooting streams of sticky burning napalm. The beautiful berry-ladened hedgerows around the base, which once beckoned all to pick and eat, were now consumed in flames. The thick greasy soot swirled around, adding to the defenders' cover. Anti-tank and personnel barriers once hidden were glowing cherry red in the bushes' absence, strategically corralling those who darted towards the front doors of the once inviting firehouse.

A phalanx of sixteen seemingly unstoppable suits advanced through the archway that Fagan so treasured. As fast as Lee Harvey got off three rounds on Kennedy, Fagan's pooka dropped the first four with deadly headshots; one too many apparently. This rookie mistake allowed the back row to decipher the location of Fagan's invisible sniper. Those remaining in this murder hole didn't scatter, they dabbed to the corner of the third tier of the pyramid. Even if he planned to hit and run, being instantly spotted by the remaining twelve angry men was just long enough for them to call down the HAARP. A bank of linked batteries in Alaska sent four million volts into space, which bounced from a multitude of satellites to blast through the translucent ceiling of New Allentown and liquify the pooka. Poor, poor pooka.

DESTINY'S CHILDREN

Fagan and Mange watched the monitors from the war room on Five.

"There are too many my boy. You must take the remaining cadets and rendezvous with Major Betty and the others."

Mange responded with tearful eyes. "Are we abandoning our dream?"

"Quite the contrary. You must evacuate with the children. They are the Gilgamesh Project. This was only a building. Now dry your yellow eyes and lead the movement. Get to the goblin."

"Surely you can escape with us."

"They will never stop now. The anomaly can't be hidden anymore. It must end here. We must set this straight."

With that, Mange turned, never to see the old man again in this life.

The librarian led forty or so of the children down the stairs. They were halted by two Red suits coming up, who tilted their heads like confused dogs following a scent momentarily lost. It was Mange's yellow eyes that gave them pause.

Ambidextrous Betty Rumble, who had given chase, swung her 12-pound sledgehammers, silencing one of the bloodhounds. As quick as the major removed her mauls from the now hourglass-shaped helmet, the other Red suit vaulted past the line of escaping children. Before she continued the hunt, Mange grabbed her wrist and said, "exodus." The lifelong bodyguard of Fagan knew and followed her directive. Turning, they continued down the staircase to freedom.

The twelve angry men marched into the silent pyramid, only to pause upon reaching the rising platform from below. There stood the Paladin flanked by six Yellow Corp suits. All the combatants drew their plasma long swords and clashed, producing such light and heat that their shadowy images were burned into the walls like ancient cave drawings.

General Blake Salim gripped the handle on his Bowie. He thought to himself, "This is a good day to . . . ."

Fagan, wearing his finest prosthetics, walked up to Six to find Winter in his Yellow Jacket showing off its features to his newly found love.

"Winter and Doora! Take the throne!"

"What is going on?" In no truer Goth harmony could this duet be mistaken.

"You're going to save humanity," Fagan revealed as he secured the newlyweds on the throne. "Mange and I have put most of the story together. Some of the details are sketchy. As far as we can figure, we have done this before. Many times in fact. I trust you to be the scout. If you feel it's too big, send the boy with the special eyes back for all of us. You are needed in the far future. Consider yourselves the last members of a relay race for the survival of humanity. Or call it Eden, the remix."

Fagan reached out his human hand, touching Doora's cheek.

"This beautiful brown skinned girl has a higher purpose in the future. You need to protect and deliver her."

Doora exploded, "Deliver me! What am I, a package? Deliver me! For a good guy, you preach some of the most offensive sermons."

"Where?" blurted Winter.

"A new age?" Fagan questioned and continued. "I couldn't figure that out. I told you the details are hazy. Apparently we need to keep doing this. That much I know. Each rerun leaves clues for us to improve black hole earth. Looks like you're going to be a father in the future somewhere. There is a statistical chance the human race is just tired of running. You just have to keep her alive and make it back eventually." Before Doora could unleash an attack fueled with the dirtiness of being left out and objectified, Fagan parried. "Look Doora, you didn't need to carry this weight. You had a job to be the best of what we had to offer. Strength, intelligence and charisma will be needed where you're going. To be honest we can't know for sure. Even if you find yourself playing the role of Eve, you are Wonder Woman. We just don't know what's on the other side of our disposable black hole. It's a one way ticket out of here. We believe this breakthrough technology scratched some universal record player. Now the record is skipping. This is where our ignorance is surpassed by our arrogant selfishness. We are holding part of the multiverse hostage. Granted, extinction is a viable excuse."

"Is it?" Responded the choir.

"Is it?" Fagan responded tiredly and continued. "You have a big decision to make. Your lifelong training to adventure has been an apprenticeship for restarting humanity."

Suddenly Doora's powder was all wet and useless.

Fagan confessed, "I raised you for this moment. I also taught you about your body, your choice. So I want you to understand that I was preaching for this moment. I trust you. If you feel that you can carry the ball for humanity, then keep your adolescent. Don't send the boy. Lift the needle. Let the record move forward. Once you land in your new time, you will have time to raise your golden child. This is where you will have to flex your skills. You must find the Goblin's throne, which will be set to send your adolescent back to start this again. Mange and I played out so many scenarios we figure your child comes back and landed thirty-three years ago as a young clueless boy. But your eyes bounced further backwards in time. Yes Winter, your boy will require your eyes. So you could argue this technology never was a red team invention."

Winter surprisingly digested this ominous prophecy with little emotional push back.

Fagan continued. "Now go to the archives in your processor under D&D."

Filled with so many questions, Winter still followed his words like commands.

Fagan quickly swung his personal backpack around and placed it on Winter's lap. Within the bag was a package of various seeds the Goblin King had prepared. Not knowing what the future actually needed for its redo, they collected as many different seeds as they could imagine, medicinal, nutritional, and biological. Fagan started to distribute the booty into each of their backpacks.

Doora said, "You think that I should carry the seeds? You are just an obvious... ugh. You are cracking jokes to the very end. And I never thanked you for distracting me because you were protecting me."

Fagan held back the leak and said, "I fear that I will be misunderstood where you're going. In the bag are two misunderstood offensive minds of their times. Darwin's Origin Of Species first edition and a vinyl record of Don Rickles, Hello Dummy. Both legends took chances and shook the world to make it better."

Winter blurted, "This isn't fair, I have so many unanswered questions!"

"UNFAIR! I did the heavy lifting! Sit back and enjoy the ride again. We have no more time here. Now open the file named Deities and Demigods. "

After complying, the throne started shaking and the lights dimmed throughout the ziggurat. Winter felt ready to pass out. Only having energy for one last question, he asked, "How can you be sure?"

Fagan turned and exited the chamber housing the throne. Looking back, he took his good finger and peeled off his right contact lens, revealing a pretty blue eye.

"Because eye know."

The throne disappeared.

The Red suit exited the staircase facing the one eyed god and paused. "I have visual on the rabbit. Scanner confirmation on the optical implants. These are the runners."

Fagan lit a Salem and said, "Mr. DeVille, I'm ready for my close-up."

"Five" by Robert V. Kilroy

The Human Virus

by Bertram Montiekowicz

It called out her name, "Evreatra."

A blur. She shifted, sad and uncomfortable, strapped flat on her back. Her vision restored, and there sat the creature. Could it be human? From its posture, demeanor, placement in relation to her, its weariness, her own sense of helplessness and violation, it must be a doctor.

Her eyes shifted, confirming suspicions, an array of medical equipment, each tube and wire bent towards her, a dripping bag flowing thick brown syrup, and somewhere in the distance, a reassuring beep. The surfaces and geometric arrangement of the room had been fabricated from a plastic like steel; it belonged on a stereotypical alien spaceship, affecting her understanding of the inhabitant.

This being, whatever it was, had roused her from a technological sleep. And for a Jazz only that last night with you, distending like a dream, seeing it for the first time through your eyes. Impossible, but there are other reasons not to leave someone in X-Stasis for too long, stranger outcomes than hers.

Evreatra tried a sentence. "I have Ardy, to heal." Her voice sounded strange, not her own, a mechanical process long idle, in need of spark, fuel, fluid.

It said, "I saw. We developed a similar technology but we call it something else. I didn't want to connect while you were unconscious."

The creature reached across her prone frame and leaned on the rail, pressing a button with its very human thumb. A fresh compartment opened on the bedrail. The doctor lifted Evreatra's lifeless hand and set it into the opening. Another press of the button and the compartment glowed red. She felt a course of power running through the metal veins strung alongside her bone and cartilage, up her arm and from the shoulder junction to the tips of her toes.

Her eyejammy activated.

In the upper right-hand corner of her vision, in red font, a blinking dash where the time and date should be, and finally, resolution, her system tracking wireless connections, finding a piece of equipment that needed to synchronize. Her eyes shifted uncontrollably. Based on the digital clock in her eyejammy, she had gone to sleep in the year 2047 only to wake in 2802.

Her other eye menus remained blank, which meant every network had either disappeared or switched to a new platform. Her health monitor held the usual details, everything stable, but it also showed her system had been approached by this same being. Making selections more with her brain than eye, she reviewed the medical credentials the doctor had entered into her system hoping to unlock it; they matched those from her time? She could see the doctor's repeated attempts blocked. That meant someone or something else had hacked their way in, disabled her security, took what it needed, covered its tracks.

Another nearly identical being popped into view, blocking the artificial light emanating from panels in the ceiling.

Evreatra recoiled in horror, moving barely an inch, a painful gesture.

The second creature stretched a smile across what might have been a mouth. "Welcome back!"

This being sounded exactly like the first, just set at different levels of friendliness; good cop, bad cop. Still talking English. Unbelievable.

A lifetime trying to handle change, control it, when the most powerful things never changed.

Calling for a power boost from Ardy allowed her to shift her head slightly but purposely to face the doctor; Ardy, the name they used for the Recharge

Docktor, relied on a purifying light to enter bodies that had been modified to pass these waves through the system. Once established Ardy would provide whatever energy her body needed most.

She asked, "Water?"

"Sure!" The other being said. It returned briefly to lift a cylinder towards her face. When it realized she couldn't move her head, its human hand grabbed the mouthpiece on top of the bottle, which extended out. It set the straw between her lips and tilted the container back. She felt the water flow.

"That's enough," the doctor said. The other withdrew out of view to set the container on a shelf.

She reset her head into the bed foam. "Who put me in X-stasis?"

The smiley one crept back into view, holding a large circular metal container.

It said, "We have your memories right here!"

"What?"

"Your memories . . . we downloaded them from your eyejammy."

The doctor said, "We watched them. We've seen what you did."

The smiling being clutched the large metal disk as it spoke. "Now, of course we didn't have time to watch everything. We had to divide it up. Whoever watched the most earned the chance to meet you if you ever woke up. That's me! I guess you could say I became a fan. I even watched the good stuff other people found. So I'm pretty familiar with like, your whole life; well, at least since you got jacked. Once we figured out a way to upload the eyejammy recordings," it held forth the cylinder for a moment, "I could search as well, and the doctor had your health data, so we could pair the two and focus on the special times, like the ones where you had a raised heart rate. All I can say is, wow."

She jutted her jaw to show there was nothing to hide. "Then you can tell me how I ended up like this."

The doctor interrupted. "We're going to be asking the questions."

She drew more power, challenging every muscle, just to eyeball them, one to the other and back. "Stand me up."

The two beings shared a look and the doctor turned his attention to the console before him. It pressed another button while spinning a white ball set into the black surface. The table rotated into a comfortable position, upright but reclined at an angle.

She said, "You can remove these restraints."

The doctor pressed a different button and the hard synthetic straps slipped below the edge of the operating table, forming part of its smooth surface.

Evreatra felt no pain from her bonds, just an itchy numbness. She still wore the stasis suit as it would be too dangerous to ever remove. Someone had placed her in X-stasis against her will and never removed her for maintenance. Evreatra tried to imagine more heartless betrayals, angry. Ardy responded with more endorphins but she used her eyejammy to adjust the settings.

After another drag on the power, she tilted her head, struggling to look at her other hand, which slowly lifted into view. As expected, the cybergenic suit had grown over and through her skin. She could only imagine how horrible her face had become, as X-stasis required special attachments for the eyes, nose, mouth, ears, access points at the temple, with a tight seal around the neck that served as a second heart, and these would need to be periodically removed, and now were simply her.

The titanium sockets on her wrists, for connecting an exoskeleton, were just as clean and sturdy as when she was last awake, tapped as they were into her very bone. A wire filament ran through her thickest marrow, an internal fiber network connecting similar sockets in her elbows and shoulders. She had sockets alongside her ankle, knee and thigh, for each legpiece, two on each side of her rib cage for the backpack, and a smaller set behind each temple access point. A final small socket at the base of her neck connected to her nervous system with a reinforced cable that dangled from the exoskeleton's headpiece.

Evreatra's misshapen head fell back into the comfortable flexfoam. "Why did you awaken me?" It came out as a long moan.

The happy one stepped back as the doctor continued its smug observation.

She writhed, but it wasn't in pain. "Put me back to sleep, please ... there is no life for me here."

The doctor said, "We broke your bed getting it open. You'll never sleep again, there's not enough of you left...."

She wanted so to close her eyes, but much of the original organic hardware had withered away, especially around the nose and cheekbone, leaving only dry unblinking cyber organics that could only be operated by command, one the hacker had disabled when it breached her firewalls. "Is this earth?"

The fan indulged. "Of course! You've never left earth!"

"How did you find me?"

The doctor said, "We're here to set up a geothermal plant. We scouted this location, well, you're the living proof, it's a durable source of continuous power. It kept you going, kept you alive."

She stared at him a long time. "You call this living?"

The doctor let go a long breath, exhausted. "I expected thanks, for giving you life again."

"It's nothing but suffering." Evreatra sank further into the form fitting foam. "Frankenstein." The beings looked at each other. "Forget it." Her anger came out as sarcasm. "I just can't wait for you to tell me what earth has become."

The fan shared a nervous look with the doctor before speaking. "Oh, well, um, it's hard to say. Our scouts wanted to make contact with any earthlings. We eventually encountered a people who claimed to be the most high-tech, so we learned what we could from them, but they couldn't tell us much about ancient history. There's not much good you can say about the last hundred years or so... you see, the magnetic pole shifted to the south, so there was no longer any protection from the sun's rays."

She looked away and the fan hesitated.

The being tried a different tact. "Don't worry, though... it's not like earth died! People just had to adapt to a sun that kills. So what did they do? They moved into caves, travelled at night. We have some locals that we trade with. Good people. They scavenge the earth you lived in for anything useful. There was so much waste back then. That's where we got this." It held out the cylinder again. "People move on. That's what we do. We're always going to find a way to survive. At this point we have to say, despite the constant threats, there's just no way to wipe us out. From what our contacts told us, even before the pole shift, earth's population started living below the sea, especially after the coastlines rose so quickly before the New Ice Age. And outerspace, too; don't forget about billionaires in space. One thing you have to say for Musk and Bezos, they built their space mansions to last."

Evreatra turned to her fan, still hanging onto its hideous smile. "You're human?"

It seemed hurt. "I guess you look at the two of us and say, what are you guys, twins? But we're not, we're really not. We're human. We changed, adapted, but we're still human, we'll always be human. Nothing can take that away from us. Don't feel sorry for me. We made it back to earth!"

The doctor asked, "We have some questions we want you to answer. Is that too much to ask? You mention Frankenstein, well we know the story. Our system has access to the greatest literature from your time. From what I understand the story is supposed to be about the dangers of trying to play God. Am I right? The way I look at it, if everyone wants to play God, I mean, look at how quick we are to judge each other, well, it must be natural. Maybe it's our desire to play God that keeps us going. And what's wrong with that? God's a good role model, isn't It? The innovators, they brought light into darkness. They gave life. Just like I did for you. You may want to be miserable, but I think I know how God must have felt, that after a great toil, here is this living, thinking being."

Ardy activated the artificial heart embedded in her neck and shoulders, and she felt a little stronger, enough to swallow.

She assumed they were running a lie detector and that's why they didn't cede control of her eyes; at least, that's how she would conduct her interrogations. She said, "You know so much about me and I don't know anything about you."

The two beings exchanged another look and the doctor glanced away, probably at a camera.

The fan spoke, "We thought, even if we could wake you, your mind would be, you know, like toast. We can't be sure how well you can access your own memories. So here goes. You probably remember our ancestors. You remember the asteroid, Alexander, I mean, who could forget that! Well, they put people in arks, remember, in case it didn't work? And the arks were flying away from earth. You remember, don't you? They had to get beyond the circle of space trash."

"Yes."

"Well, then you definitely remember the ark that disappeared, people thought it stumbled into a stargate. Well that was us, well not us, but our ancestors! We were on the Liberty. You remember our ship don't you? In your memories you were really worried, everybody was, but they were safe. It was just some alien race playing a prank. They thought it would be a good time to have some fun, you know the type, so they sent our ancestors off into outerspace; it's kind of funny but you have to think of it the right way! Well, that was our ancestors, they were humans just like everyone else, picked for the ark precisely because their genetic diversity offered them the best chance to survive the longest. You remember how the arks were built. You remember what it was like during the asteroid, everyone working together. If the asteroid was a world killer, we on the arks, we had to last long enough to return to earth and start again. And miracle of miracles, here we are! We survived. Whoo-hoo! And where the aliens left us, it wasn't that far from earth, really, once you know how to travel that fast. We were close enough to hear radio transmissions from earth. Well, not at first, there was a delay, so it was a while before we heard the first radio transmission . . . oh, I should ask you, do you know what it was? The first radio transmission we heard? You don't know? The radio transmission farthest from earth is Adolph Hitler inviting the nations of the world to the 1936 Olympics. So we heard that, but then there was another long delay, but you have to understand, for our ancestors, when the first radio waves came through, they were so happy to get anything from home. It made them feel like maybe we weren't that far away after all. That maybe if they could hang on, earth would develop the technology to reach them. Of course our ancestors were most interested in the time after the Liberty disappeared, waiting to find out what happened, whether earth had survived the asteroid. Talk about a cliff-hanger! But that was it, after the asteroid we never heard another radio broadcast, so what else could we do? All these years, we assumed the worst."

Evreatra felt tears would make her feel better, but even the thought of sadness brought such a painful tightening of the semisynthetic skin around her eyes she had to turn away from her feelings and think about something neutral, for which she felt only boredom.

The doctor broke his silence. "Now you understand. Your memories are the first real evidence we have about the times that followed the asteroid. I can't tell you the disappointment, I can't put it into words. Our ancestors had made every sacrifice, fearful that humanity itself relied upon our survival, and meanwhile back home everyone had simply returned to the same old petty differences. The other arks just landed and everybody went back to their old life."

Evreatra asked, "Where did you find my bed?"

The fan seemed far from talked out. "We're miners! We came back to earth because the magnetic pole has finally switched north. It's safe for humanity to come out of its caves again. What a great time to be alive! Plenty of wide open spaces. Nothing but opportunity. We're supposed to be setting up a geothermal generator and look at what we've been doing instead!"

Her mind raced with possibilities. "Someone buried me in the earth and just left me there?"

"Not just you. There's a bunch of beds down there."

"What?"

"Yeah, unreal."

"How many others have you awoken?"

The doctor interrupted. "You're the first and I'm assuming you'll be the last. We received special authorization to raise one of you, because of the unique historic value; I mean, it's every archaeologists' dream, isn't it? To have a dialogue with their discovery? I should let you know our conversation is being recorded."

"How many beds did you find?

The nice one, still smiling, said, "More than a hundred, but we're still counting. They're all interconnected, well except yours, you were the first one we found. This place must have cost mucho cash. We have to take our time down there. We found a trap, it was like a blast room. The walls were painted with nanothermite and the floor designed to throw off a spark. We had to pass through this chamber to get to the tomb. I mean, it's not like we have the right personnel or equipment for any of this. We're totally unprepared!"

Evreatra pushed her elbows into the foam, trying to lean forward. Her eyes clicked into place, locking on the doctor. "What do you want from me?"

"You fought in the Second America Civil War. We want you to create a record, a deposition."

She slumped again. "Well you can forget it. I'm not going to participate."

The nice one interrupted. "Don't look at it that way. Why not? Why not tell your story? Up until an hour ago we assumed we could never reach you. We're not sure how long you have."

The doctor remained undeterred. "We have every right to ask you questions, don't you think? We spent considerable time and energy getting you to this point. I want to get in some questions while I still can. Now just, please cooperate for the record."

"If you watched my memories you already know everything." She wanted to scream but her diaphragm ached. "What is the point of all this?" She rested her unsettling eyes on the other being, who clutched the metal can. "I just want to go back to sleep. If I die I die."

The fan seemed hurt. "Don't say that!"

The doctor said, "It's something, isn't it? We, who lost our way from earth so long ago, have returned to make such an important discovery. Our ancestors must have wanted to be part of history, otherwise why volunteer for the ark? Why suffer through the trials of space camp? They left us their diaries. We remember them fondly. That is why we roused you from your long sleep. By acting in this way, we join our ancestors, who struggled and sacrificed because they knew that is how to become part of history."

Evreatra asked, "Why won't you tell me how I ended up like this?"

The other said, "I wish we could say for sure!"

The being pulled the metal cylinder into two pieces, carrying the lid back on the table set against the wall. Evreatra craned her neck to follow the creature, noting some pieces of her exoskeleton standing on the same surface. The creature presented the open can; inside, a black reel of tape.

Evreatra asked, "What the Trump is this?"

The doctor said, "This was the only format we could convert them to. Your bed was so old, and we couldn't find any reference point for some of the equipment. There's a lot of proprietary technology in play down there. From what we can tell, the systems are still running. There's a network. Also, our sounding equipment indicates there are other chambers below, but we have no way to reach them."

She asked, "You put my memories on tape?"

The creature shrugged. "You have to understand the predicament our ancestors were in when they were left alone in an unknown corner of blank space, with no more than a dying sun to sustain their days."

Evreeta did not feel tired, just weary, and her body shifted, lugubrious. She said, "If you watched my memories then you should know how I ended up here."

They looked at each other. The doctor said, "We'll tell you what we know. You went to sleep one night. That was your last memory. You were a soldier in the war. Each of you had a little room in an underground bunker. The coordinates match. You never left that bunker. From what we can tell the tomb was built about a year before you first retreated into the bunker."

The fan said, "I can add to that, too, you know, when we're done. We just got some other memories down on tape. I was watching them when they said you were showing signs of life. Believe it or not our tech support guy wants to write over your memories as we're out of tape but I told them this was like a museum piece."

Evreatra swallowed hard, trying to occupy the reaches of her mind that had lain dormant so long they lost their relevancy, but which she knew were the best parts in life. There was something good hidden, a strong bonded family that loved each other, before the Civil War tore them apart, shouting matches over the Thanksgiving Day dinner table, fistfights on the Fourth of July.

She nodded towards the table. "You removed my XO."

The doctor said, "Tech support said there was no other way to bypass your internal systems."

"I'll need it to move around."

The doctor said, "Yeah, we're not sure about that, you know, for your own safety. You've been in stasis so long . . . it's dangerous, don't you think, trying to take on the extra load?"

"You're wrong. I can leave my hand in. I'm wired for that." Evreatra used her head to gesture towards the tubes dripping somewhere into her system. "If you let me power up my legs you can disconnect me from whatever this is. Those leg units were designed to regulate bodily functions so you won't need any of these connections. You have my full suit?"

The fan said, "Yeah, we have all your stuff right here." It stepped to the table, setting the reel of tape down and returning the lid. Evreatra leaned on an elbow for a better view. The fan said, "Arms, legs, backpack. Whatever this is." It held up a simple shotgun.

She had never used a shotgun before, preferring something more high tech that could tap into her system, to make her aim true, a weapon smarter than herself, to coordinate the killing. The more technology between yourself and the actual death-dealing, the easier it is to fall asleep that night. These weapons relied on precise munitions and demanding power sources. Unlike these other devices, Evreatra knew how to make ammunition for this weapon. She nodded appreciatively and said, "I've never used it before. I know it makes a distinctive sound, and people called it the peacemaker for just that reason."

"Oh, that sounds nice."

The doctor seemed disinterested. "Are you going to tell us what we want to know?"

Evreatra said, "Let's make a deal. Give me have my legs. My legs will help me heal. They're personalized to know exactly what I need. The better I feel, the more cooperative I become. What do you say? At least let me watch my own memories, as you both have done."

"You can't do that!"

The doctor said, "They won't let you."

Evreatra took a long look around the room. "Who is They?"

The doctor made a sound that must have been laughter. "Who's They? Who's always They? They's that got the power. How do you think we got back to earth? We were brought here by an alien race, our benefactors, the Kafk."

The happy one said, "Come on, just tell us what you remember about the Rainbow War, the Reds and the Blues, the Yellows."

The freakish being seemed disconnected with the content. Evreatra's memories, not the ones on tape but the ones in her mind, held no happiness. She watched the gulf spread between her and this being: she, who had suffered, watching people bleed to death and die, listening to them moan, and another, who simply watched those same people die on a screen, muted, after fast forwarding through the meaningless hours of her day. Maybe she didn't want to review her life. "It was nothing to smile about."

The doctor said, "I told him or her that. Why not simply answer our questions? Let's just focus on the Whites. They did not want to be affiliated with any color, I get that, but what did they stand for? We watched the memories, but . . ."

"What are you asking me for? You've seen it all."

"These Grays, they hated the Blues and the Reds?"

"We didn't hate anything but the stupid war. We hated anyone who would pit one American against another, as it was always either for political or monetary gain, or both."

The doctor said, "Why join Gray? You didn't seem to fit in at all."

"If you've seen my memories you know why I became a Gray."

The happy one said, "Tech support thinks your memory files might have been altered."

She paused to reflect so the being continued.

"Yeah, he or she thinks, like, fake memories were added to fill in the gaps at certain critical points. He or she is still trying to figure it out, but there's a lot going on right now."

The doctor said, "For example, we could not find any memories of you and Swinson. You were on stage during his speeches, but you never met? He was the leader of the Whites, and yet you never spoke to him once?"

She asked, "What do you think, he came around and talked to everyone personally? You're pretty naïve. You think the people on stage are important when a politician is talking? I told you already, I never did anything special. You've seen my memories."

The doctor said, "We thought it a little strange."

"I'm sure transferring this data onto tape has nothing to do with it." She tried to sit up again. "Look, give me my arms and legs and at least I can stand up. I feel lifeless right now. You want answers, I'll answer any question you might have. Let me suit up and I'll tell you whatever you want to know."

They shared a look and the weary doctor gave a short nod. They began disconnecting her from the apparatus. The happy one went over to the table and grabbed the right leg. With its metal design it looked heavier than it was. The legs stood on their own, and the being placed first one and then the other on the metal floor in front of where her operating table seemed to hover.

Evreatra lifted her repulsive foot and set it into the space provided, amazed at the technology that allowed not just her mind and body to survive the times, but also the equipment she needed.

Once her toes were in place the prosthetic activated, the heat from her body and its electric system enough to kick start the robotic processes. It sensed the power source in the Recharge Docktor and began moving the necessary wattage across her internal wiring, which was trained to displace the heat generated in a uniform fashion along her internal wiring. She found this warming sensation quite pleasant. The leg completed its first diagnostic check, the batteries designed molecule by molecule to survive the test of time, repair each other. The exoskeleton took a long moment, making its own calculations. Satisfied, the plugs adjusted into place before inserting themselves into the sockets, first at the ankle, then the knee, and finally, in her thigh. The connection with the exoskeleton came as a rush. Each socket employed numerous linkages into her frame, veins, muscles, cartilage, where organic material had been replaced with synthetic long before she went into stasis. She could feel the strength from the machine and easily lifted her other foot into place, where the process repeated. The legs took a final drag from Ardy before she pulled her hand free from the operating table.

Evreatra could do nothing but stand tall, towering over them like some swaggering monster.

Her eyejammy registered a new item, it said, COMPLETE XO DRESS. She selected and the drop down showed the missing components: ARMS, BACKPACK, HEADSET, CABLE LINK.

Swaying, unsteady, she threatened to topple. "Give me my arms!"

The being hurriedly complied. Evreatra slipped her right hand into the gauntlet and the equipment set itself as before, plugs aligning and then settling into sockets up her arm, first on one side, then the other. The rush came again, this time accompanied by the sensation the exoskeleton's arms and legs were in communication, sharing data, diagnostics, plans. Her eyejammy updated accordingly. She couldn't resist flexing each limb in turn, her resemblance to Claymation unmistakable. The metal feet seemed planted in place, while an unsteady upper body depended on the gyroscopic balancers in the robotic arms.

She set her arms into place and rotated her torso. "Can you see how to connect the backpack?"

"Yes!" The fan grabbed a rectangular piece from the table and squared it against her back. Each arm connected on the back shoulder while the legs set into the seat below the waist.

Evreatra tested the flexibility again, pleased. She took her first step.

"You're walking!"

The doctor began clicking a screen in his console.

Evreatra twisted her mechanical frame and took another step, this time in the direction of the table containing her headpiece.

The happy being said, "It's a miracle!"

She hefted the shotgun, opened and closed it in one motion to confirm it was loaded, and clipped it onto the exoskeleton.

She turned to face them both. "You want to know about the war? I'll tell you. I'll tell you. It was the stupidest war ever. It was a modern war, which is an oxy-moron, right? Progress, it just means everything gets bigger, not better. And so is it any surprise the most modern of wars was based on the biggest of lies, lies that anyone could refute with five minutes and the internet."

The doctor continued to take notes. He said, "Would you say this reflected the mentality of the Yellows as well?"

She made a quick movement, to see if she could. "I personally could not have cared less about any of it. I never even voted. I didn't have a political bone in my body. I never got involved in any of that. Every time I heard Red and Blue argue, it sounded like they were both wrong, like they were on some high school debate team, just trying to win the argument. They would twist themselves with pretzel logic, both to make accusations and to defend their own. I always wondered, what are these sides? How can one country have sides? To this day I'll always believe there were more people like me than there were either of them."

The doctor kept tapping, "Go on."

She tested the motion again, as if she needed to quickly draw the shotgun and fire. With her eye menu she clicked on MASSAGE and the exoskeleton began to move of its own accord, soothing and stretching her long idle limbs.

She said, "Here was the problem. Both the Reds and the Blues had a fringe element, and this was nothing new, that element of society has always existed, and not just in America. I'm sure it exists today. Doomsayers are the biggest egomaniacs, as they convince themselves the end of the world will be in their lifetime. These fringe elements are always trying to make some kind of last stand . . . then when the alien conspiracy turned out to be true, well, that was it. Game on."

The doctor squirmed in his seat. "So who would you say is to blame?"

Evreatra rocked her horribly adapted head on the synthetic muscles of her second heart. "I guess a lot of it goes back to the political parties and big media, and their ability to use computers to target voters and consumers. The parties would raise donations from their supporters and then give it to the media, and then the media would make it seem like the politicians were the only ones who could ever save us from all the complicated problems they themselves had created."

The beings continued to stare, the only sound the careful swirl of the exoskeleton as it prepared her body for action. After a pause she felt no need to break, the doctor said, "And?"

She stared into those eyes, so like a human, even more than her own. "And what?"

The happy being said, "We just want to understand it, you know."

"I just told you. It wasn't about territory or race or language, it was ideology. There's always going to be somebody who profits, and someone else who gets left behind, and it doesn't take long to figure out one is at the expense of the other."

The doctor finished the entry. "Just to be clear, you blame the political parties?"

She sat on the question for a moment. "Well, that's not fair, I suppose. They came up with the colors, made everything about us and them. They wanted a divided country because it was good for elections, donations. A lust for everything, but what both parties wanted most was to remain in power. They both served their largest contributors, and had to disguise their corruption by starting a culture war, pointing to differences among the American people, assuming that as long as people had lies on their lips and hate in our heart, the next election was secure. The more political the candidate, the more he portrayed himself as a culture warrior, the more electable he became, but these charlatans were terrible governors. When Asteroid Alexander came along the entire political establishment had to be shoved to the side. They were totally useless, a barrier to the collective."

The happy one said, "But when we left we thought that was all in the past."

"You mean you thought history stopped? It doesn't work that way."

The doctor said, "So just go right back to fighting."

"Of course." She stared at the being for a long moment. "Of course. These extremes from the right and left. A lot of them thought the asteroid was fake news anyway. They used it as a queue, it was like another January Six. What a mess. Bands of murderers venturing out into the American heartland. In Cold Blood was their motto, their Bible, their handbook. They struck at random, Helter Skelter. The more carnage the better. The Reds blamed the Blues, just like the Blues had blamed the Reds for their extremists. Each side convinced the other that this slim percentage of the population, one trying to end the world in rapture, the other in chaos, that they instead represented the tens of millions of votes each color earned in the last election."

They were quiet for a second, then the doctor asked, "Why fight if you felt this way?"

She turned the massage off, reaching her arms above her head, nearly touching the ceiling, before resetting into place. "What difference does it make?" She looked over at the table. "I should put on my headset." She took a robotic step towards the table.

"Wait," the doctor said.

She turned to him for a long glare. "You're awful naïve you know."

"You keep saying that; what do you mean?"

"These Kafk, your benefactors, they have faster than light travel, right? They knew how to get to earth, obviously. Did you ever think it might have been them that played the prank on the ark? Sent your ancestors off into outerspace, left them alone, feeding them just the sound waves they wanted you to hear, and then cutting them off right when they were most vulnerable? Then when the Kafk come along, you're desperate, ready to make any deal, leave home forever just to work in a mine. You're happy to kiss their feet while they play the role of benefactor; my ass."

With that she stepped to the table. Her gauntleted hands hefted the black helmet, clicking it into the backpack below and then up around her head. In her eyejammy, the addition of the headset introduced a new series of commands and data, most of which involved the materials of the room and their suitability as weapons, what amount of force or pressure would be needed to destroy or puncture everything visible. She ignored the targeting information, for now. One step remained to complete the exoskeleton, INSERT LINK CABLE. She looked around the table, but it wasn't there. She chose FIND CABLE.

She turned her helmeted head towards the two beings. "All these soldiers down there . . . how could we possibly have been captured in this way?"

The fan stayed close. "I wanted to know the same thing! That's what I was saying. I just watched the last memories of a couple of the others. I couldn't find them taking you, but I did see them take someone else. It seems there were two groups, one like yourself, who they drugged, and another that were in on it, so to speak. I count a leader, at least four handlers, as I call them, as they had a little stretcher they used to carry the bodies out of the cells. The elevator had a secret panel, and that gave them access to the lower level. They had a full medical team living down there, we got one of their memories today. It shows them getting their final instructions from the leader."

Her head swiveled into position. "Leader? Swinson is here?"

"No! Sorry, I use the term leader because there was obviously someone in charge." The happy being could not suppress a laugh. "Swinson's been dead almost as long as you've been asleep!"

"What happened to him?"

"The medical team watched the whole thing play out live on a screen. The united peoples of the world, as they called themselves, decreed the Grays must die, and they started a countdown, so Swinson surrendered, hoping he could avert a massacre. They knew Swinson spent all his money, like three-point-five billion, but on what, right? Now we know. The torture experts thought they could get him to talk eventually, but they never got their chance. The Reds stormed the courthouse and carried him out to the mob. You couldn't really recognize him when they were done. That's when the rest of the Grays vowed never to come out of the bunker. The only way to break the stalemate was to use a small nuclear bomb, but the tomb where you slept was outside the blast zone, like whoever built the place knew precisely how many megatons would be employed. The medical team did one last check on the beds and then they put themselves under. It must have been a perfect place to hide because of the radiation. There was no way to check to see if there were any survivors, but how could there be? The place was off limits, really until now."

"How long after I was taken was the bunker destroyed?"

"Maybe like nine months."

She tried to remember the day she had been taken. "You say you watched my memories. The day I was taken . . . did someone say something about picnickers?"

"Yeah, something about the number of picnickers. What does that even mean?"

"You must have skipped that memory. When somebody signed up to be a Gray it was for life. Anybody that felt different, the quitters, we called them picnickers. Like their life was a picnic."

"And then you said you would look into it, or something like that."

"That's right. So that probably moved me up the list. They figured I'd blow the lid off their little scheme."

The fan seemed excited to talk about the memories it had watched. "The whole thing must have been on Swinson's orders. He must have ordered them to put you in the bed, but first to wipe his private remarks from your eyejammy."

The suit kept her from falling flat on her face. "Why would he do such a thing?"

"We think maybe, maybe he took his inspiration from Mosada; do you know the story? In that one the besieged killed themselves, here it wasn't suicide... well, I guess you have to make that call."

She clenched her gauntleted fist and bent at the knee. "Who is this leader you keep talking about?"

"Her name is Carlson."

"Why not just make a tape of her memories?"

"Well, that's the thing, her bed remains inaccessible. The way the other beds are stacked in there makes it impossible to access her, which is weird because she must have went in last. When we discovered the tomb, the Kafk had to take the spaceship and go back to the Liberty and let them know. They're putting together a much larger team, they should be here any day now. We definitely need an explosives expert."

Her eye returned to the exoskeleton menu. The sensors had located the cable in a nearby room. She motioned toward the fan. "I'm looking for a small cable, it's meant to connect my nervous system to the exoskeleton."

The doctor said, "Tech support took it."

"Can you get it for me, please?"

The doctor waved at the other being, who walked up to one of the walls and pushed a button that caused the chamber to open. It stepped through and the door closed, but Evreatra got a whiff of the mining station, sweat and tar.

Alone, the doctor said, "Tech support wanted to study it further. We don't have much on these neck jacks. What's the purpose of it?"

"I'll show you."

The fan returned. "Tech support wasn't there, but luckily for you I found it laying on a table."

She took the cable from the being and sank one end into the headpiece. The eye command indicated READY. Relying on the guidance system, she carefully paired the other end of the cable with the jack in her neck and jammed it in. She waited the microsecond for the switch in her brain to integrate her eye menu with the circuits in the headset. As the seconds unfolded the menus all came up blank again, they were trying to find satellites, terrestrial stations, any broadcasters, but each system had rolled over, nothing available. Another second passed, searching, blinking, the full authentication provided by the connection, new code activating only because her identity could not be faked. She sensed the signal coming from the tomb.

The menu item said, EXECUTE COMMAND.

Her eye could not resist dropping the menu.

SECURE FACILITY

ACTIVATE ROBOTS

REFRESH MEDICAL TEAM

REFRESH SOLDIERS

Without issuing any commands, she browsed the new data, creating a list of the people in the tomb and sorting it by how much time they had spent in her presence. The names of her closest associates scrolled by, with Bunni at the top and Carlson and the others below. She could see that some of the beds were no longer accessible on the network because they had been tampered with by these beings.

The doctor watched her carefully. "Are you all right."

"Yes, I'm fine. You were asking about the neck jack. One of the more interesting applications involved converting the body itself into a signal tower of sorts."

"Really?" The doctor made some quick notations.

Her headset alerted her the room's far wall had a moving panel, but only when it activated.

The wall slid out of the way, becoming a window. She could see an alien creature beyond, tall and gaunt, multi-limbed and capped with a bug-like carapace. Her system could not match it to any known alien. She tried to see even further, the headset building maps of the facility as her vision extended in the room and corridor beyond the window.

A screeching sound entered the room through a speaker in the ceiling. The undiscernible language did not employ a tongue.

The doctor said, "The Kafk welcomes you."

Evreatra nodded in the alien's direction, lifting one hand in the familiar no-contact greeting adopted during the pandemics.

The alien returned the gesture with the three mandibles on its right side. It made another sound, continuing its screech as the doctor translated. The happy being seemed to understand the language as well, nodding along.

Through the translator the alien said, "Please allow me to introduce myself. I am proud to say I am the first of my kind to visit earth. I am the sole proprietor in charge of this mining operation, which includes 37 humans in various roles. In our travels, our race, the Kafk, encountered the humans from the ark named Liberty when they had already found a way to survive several generations on their own. It became clear they would soon go extinct due to a lack of genetic originality. This lack of diversity had doomed the descendants of the ark. We offered to help, and the humans accepted our help, as they understood this was the only way they could survive. These beings convinced us to reinvest in earth, and that is why we are here. We have traveled to earth in a craft capable of faster than light speed. We immediately began operations. These operations ceased with your discovery. We are happy to see that you are making such a speedy recovery, and also that you have been so forthcoming about the Civil War and your role in it. Can you focus your recollections on the violence, why there was a need for so much violence? It is a concept we are unfamiliar with, as we have never known war."

The fan said, "Yes, the violence, the violence! What was it like to kill so many people?"

She craned her synthetic neck this way and that. "What are your plans for me?"

The alien seemed to understand English as it immediately began to screech a reply. "It's not for us to decide. Our actions in this regard are governed by the Kafk Administrado, which ultimately has authority when it comes to how we will best exploit this important historic discovery."

"Am I free to go?"

The translation came soon enough. "For your own benefit and safety you should remain confined to our mining colony and we particularly urge you to remain here in the medical facility until the doctor says you are ready to venture forth. Earth is a much different place than the one you left behind, it's changed in ways that must be hard to imagine. It's likely you will not recognize much of what you see. It would be irresponsible for us to simply let you face the world alone after seven hundred and fifty-five years. Obviously, the ethical questions about reviving you have been numerous and complex."

Evreatra took a robotic step in the doctor's direction, bringing her almost next to where it still sat. She said, "I'm ready to tell you what the Grays believed in."

They both leaned forward.

She said, "We decided humanity didn't deserve to exist."

The doctor tapped the new data into his notepad. "And tell us, how do you feel now?"

She rested her gauntleted hand on the shotgun. She could see which surfaces could be penetrated and to what extent if the weapon would be fired, and at which distance. She said, "Now I feel differently. I think what I would like to do most is help the human race. The hatred I felt, the violence that resulted, that was then; this is now. I can see Swinson planning this out, leaving an army in the earth, to see it brought back to life at a time when earth is fragile, that maybe a hundred dedicated troops could change a future world in a way we never could in our own time. He knew I would never agree to such a plan. None of us would. So he did it anyway. And now here we are. And earth is there for the plucking. But it's precisely this fragility that makes me feel the way I do. I will raise the army. I will tell them to follow me. Those dark days are behind us now. As you said, to survive means we must move on."

A siren went off in their room, and she could see more blinking lights in the corridor behind the alien. The beings looked around, wondering what could possibly cause such alarm.

She said, "We decided humanity didn't deserve to live."

The doctor tapped the new data into his notepad. "And tell us, how do you feel now?"

Over their heads the speaker replayed the Alien voice, but this time the doctor did not translate. He listened, his brow in knots, while the fan's face darkened, looking from one to the other.

She prepared herself for what came next, but the doctor seemed unafraid. The Alien halted, and the doctor spoke. "The Kafk used its second brain to review our conversation. It cannot believe that you, with your hatred of humanity, would impose your view of right and wrong on the Kafk, an ancient race that has sought to spread peace and harmony throughout the universe. How dare you make such accusations with no evidence? No more evidence than it's what you would have done."

Evreatra had never been one given to much introspection. At this moment, she felt the responsibility of those who had sacrificed everything for the cause, and now it was her that held the power, to bring peace to earth finally, the only way it seemed possible, by ending the human experiment.

She said, "I think it's time to meet the troops."

Made in the USA
Coppell, TX
11 January 2023

10811567R00118